Dumplings and Disaster:
Alphabet Soup Mysteries

Book 4

Erica J Whelton

Publisher: Sunseri Design Publishing
Cover Designer: Mariah Sinclair Book Cover Design
ISBN: 978-1-956069-30-3

Printed in the United States of America

This is dedicated to all the military veterans and active-duty members – From a fellow veteran

Books in this series:

Appetizers and Alibis (Book 1)
Biscuits and Bodies (Book 2)
Cornbread and Coffins (Book 3)
Dumplings and Disaster (Book 4)
Eclairs and Executions (Book 5)
Falafels and Fatalities (Book 6)
Gumbo and Grudges (Book 7)

Other books by this author:

Paranormal Cozy Mystery
Premedicated Murder: Medium with a Heart (book 1)
Replicated Murder: Medium with a Heart (book 2)
Organized Murder: Medium with a Heart (book 3)
Inherited Murder: Medium with a Heart (book 4)
Crafted Murder: Medium with a Heart (book 5)
Destined Murder: Medium with a Heart (book 6)

Small-town Women's Fiction
Mandy's Story: Courage – Finding Herself Series (book 1)
Becca's Story: Purpose – Finding Herself Series (book 2)
Caroline's Story: Serenity – Finding Herself Series (book 3)

The Haunting of Anna-Rose (Paranormal Suspense)
Decoding Us (Women's Fiction/Friendship)

Chapter One

I was working in the kitchen, prepping the soup of the day. Today we were offering vegetable beef. I'd made it a month ago on a whim and it became one of the most requested items.

Cullen, my assistant manager, suggested we advertise on social media to get the word out.

"That way, the customers know which soup we are serving that day. Plus, we can hype up our other menu items," he had said.

I couldn't disagree, but I was never good at keeping up on socials. Sometimes I would waste time scrolling through them, but I rarely posted much myself.

"Who would run it?" I asked.

"I will. If you're good with the idea, that is?"

"You think you can keep up with it?"

"Yes, not a problem. I did it in my past job."

I had to think about it for all of half a second because I could see nothing negative about his idea. It could only help with business.

"Okay, then I say go for it."

We probably should have been doing this all along, but sometimes the most obvious things weren't obvious until someone pointed them out.

Thank goodness for Cullen and his fresh take on things.

That was a week ago, and it was already having a positive response from the community and was bringing in business from other cities.

When I would do my rounds to greet customers, they made a point to tell me they were from Pinehurst or Camden or Wisteria. I even had some from Houston and New York come in.

"How did you find us?" I asked.

"Social media. A friend shared pictures and we just had to come check it out," the New Yorker had said.

"And we saw you on the Food Network several times," his fellow traveler added.

It was so much fun to talk to them all.

Now, I was finding myself going online and engaging with customers that way. It was energizing. Sure, there were the negative comments that were like a gut punch, but then I'd see a picture of smiling faces or read some kind words, and I could get past the bad review.

My friends, Sawyer and Vee, who were also my roommates, loved the soup last time I made it. So tonight, I planned to take enough home for dinner along with a half dozen biscuits and another half a dozen cornbread muffins. Just a perk of being the boss and owner.

Noah came in while I was dicing the carrots.

"Mornin'." He stopped at my station, watching me for a moment. "Wow, that always amazes me to see you chop so quickly."

"Ha, yeah, I guess I'm quick. Learned it by doing so many competitions." I kept the blade slicing through the vegetable as I smiled. "Oh, and good morning."

"Veggie beef today?"

"Yep. It just sounded good. Plus, I stopped at the farmers' market yesterday. I got a ton of great stuff." I thumbed towards the table behind me where I had set all the boxes I'd bought.

He walked over, examining the goods, picking up a bit of dill to smell it.

"I love the smell of dill," he said. "By the way, did you hear about that building that burned down the day before yesterday?"

"Um, no, which one?"

While most of Dashwood was beautiful and thriving, there were parts of town, like the neighborhood I had grown up in, not being maintained at all. The areas have been almost abandoned, which made them perfect to be renovated. That's just what one city council committee was working on.

"That one near where Earl used to live, on Jamison."

"Oh, that one?"

It had been abandoned since I was a teenager. They were planning to make that into some luxury apartments with shops and restaurants on the first floor. A lot of people were excited about it.

"Yeah."

I threw the carrots into the pot, giving it a stir. "What happened?"

"Don't know, but they found a body inside."

"Really?"

Better them than me. I was tired of finding dead bodies. I have already found two and been involved in three murder investigations. More than what I had ever thought I would see in my life.

"Yeah, they aren't sure who he is, but some said he was a homeless veteran."

"That's sad. I wonder if he has family somewhere."

"No idea. It wasn't on the news." He tapped my station before heading to the office.

After he left, I thought about that poor man. I knew nothing about him, only what Noah had said. However, I knew some military veterans. In fact, I had two working for me, Marco and Smokes. Marco was a busser and Smokes did the dishes.

Marco had retired from the Marines after twenty-five years. His wife, Selene, was a teacher at Dashwood elementary school, and he had two grown children.

He always had a positive attitude and a fun energy. He could be found joking with the other employees or telling jokes to customers.

Then there was Smokes who retired after twenty years in the Army. He was divorced, with four grown children and two grandchildren. He was a quieter guy, keeping more to himself, but he thanked me often for the job.

"Washing dishes takes little brain power. I love it," he'd said, many times.

I'm glad that they loved it so much. We enjoyed them both being here, and I felt really lucky to have such hard-working employees.

Slowly, more and more employees came in for the day. Some were also talking about the abandoned building.

Marco came in, shuffling over, flashing me a weak smile. His energy felt heavy, and his eyes looked red and puffy. It wasn't like him to look so down.

"You okay?"

"Did you hear about the building over on Jamison?" he asked me.

"I did."

"The guy was a friend of mine." His voice cracked.

"Oh, gosh, I am so sorry."

"Yeah, thanks. I'm just sorry I couldn't help him get the assistance he needed. Counseling, a job, and a safe place to live." Marco hung his head. "We bonded over our military service. He had some demons and so do I."

"You do?"

He looked at me with a weak smile. "You know what they say about the sad clown?" He shrugged, then went to get to work.

I watched him prepping his cleaning supplies. My heart broke for him. I wanted to ask him more questions about his friend, but we had to finish getting ready for the day. We would open in just fifteen more minutes.

I watched him shuffle out of the kitchen into the dining room.

Sad clown indeed, but I could understand why.

We got all our setup done just in time for the early lunch crowd. They came in fast and hungry, and in a blink it was 2 pm.

"Chef, the soup is popular today," Hannah said as she put two more in the window, yelling for a runner.

I smiled. I just knew it would be. I'd have to remember to check our social media accounts later to see any reviews or feedback.

"Good day today, I think." Hannah said. "We sold at least one of everything on the menu. I changed the paper in my ticket machine twice."

"Nice. I changed mine once. I guess you win."

We laughed.

"What can I say? Your soup is popular."

We began cleaning our stations. Anytime we weren't cooking, we were cleaning and prepping and cleaning again. I could almost hear my old culinary arts instructor, Duncan Jones's, lesson on cleaning.

"If you clean as you go, you'll have less to do in the end."

I also liked the phrase, *'if you have time to lean, you have time to clean.'* I like it so much that I had a poster made, and it is hanging over the door leading to the dining room. It was visible to the entire kitchen there.

There was a loud commotion coming from the dining room. I exchanged looks with Hannah. Her eyes were wide as she shrugged.

Noah came jogging out of the office as I was drying my hands to go check out what was happening. We spoke at the same time.

"What in the world?"

"What's happening?"

We stepped into the dining room to find the police were here, and they had Marco in handcuffs.

It was Officers Kyle "Raff" Rafferty and Lupe Perez. I'd gone to school with both of them. Raff saw me and gave me a head nod.

"What is happening?" I asked.

They exchanged a look. Perez nodded.

"We're arresting him for murder," Raff said, flatly.

"Murder? Murder of who?"

Marco was stoned faced as he looked at me. "They think I murdered Zachary, my friend. The homeless vet I mentioned."

"Oh, my. There's no way," I said. "You couldn't have."

"We have CCTV footage of him going into the building. Not long after he left, it was on fire."

Well, that didn't sound good.

I studied my employee. This didn't feel right. I just had a gut feeling he had nothing to do with it. He wasn't that type of person. Okay, so I had used him a few times as a sort of security guard. He was a large guy and had an authoritative vibe, but I couldn't picture him actually killing anyone. Then again, my father had been my hero, loving and caring until the night he killed a man.

Plus, I hadn't known about the sad clown part until today. What could he be hiding behind that smile and the sad eyes? Sad eyes I only noticed this morning.

Bleep, I guess anything was possible, but looking into Marco's face, I just knew he hadn't done it.

"Don't worry, Chef. I will be okay." He nodded and let the officers lead him away.

We all stood there watching as they left. I looked around. This should not be happening. I had to do something, but what?

Without thinking, I ran out the front door, following them.

"Wait, Raff," I called out.

He turned, studying me. He looked over at Perez. "Give me a second."

She nodded as she loaded Marco into the back of the car.

Raff jogged over to me.

"What's up?" He smiled.

"Is there anything I can do to help? I just can't ... I can't believe he would do this."

Raff frowned. "I don't know what I believe. He has always seemed like a good guy, but the evidence is pretty damning."

"It sounds like it."

Rafferty gave a nod before joining Perez in the car. I watched helplessly as they drove Marco away. I don't know how long I stood there, frozen in disbelief and fear, but jumped when a hand touched me.

"Sorry, Chef," Noah said. "I was just checking on you."

"I can't believe this."

Noah slowly turned to face me. "Are you going to help him?"

I thought about the past several months. I had managed to solve three crimes, murders. What was one more?

"Yeah, of course."

I just needed to figure out what he knew and get more information about his homeless friend. It would have to wait until he wasn't in police custody. None of them would like it if I got involved, but too bad. Marco was one of my best employees and I wouldn't allow him to be wrongly convicted, even if now it was just a gut feeling.

Chapter Two

I woke up early. Too early. The last two days raced through my mind. Marco had been arrested for murder. Murder of someone he claimed to be his friend. I believed he didn't, but I had no way yet to prove otherwise.

Mostly because I hadn't gotten to talk to him yet, but today was the day. He had been released from jail yesterday, after posting bail, and would be back at work.

With his absence, I was down to only one busser on day shift. I had two more, but they were on the night shift. Noah had suggested we stagger their shifts to help. The only problem, Andy was in school, and Neal's wife worked, so he couldn't come in until she was home to stay with their children.

Between the food runners and the servers, we had made it work the last few days, but if Marco got tied up in a lengthy trial, we would have to hire someone new. We couldn't go long without another person.

Heck, we probably needed to hire extra employees anyway, as we would get so busy sometimes that it was difficult to keep up with tables and the servers would start bussing to fill the gaps.

I flopped over to my stomach and stared at my clock. Why did I want to be my own boss? I just wanted to cook. It was the thing that brought me the most joy.

I was extremely thankful for my managers, Noah and Cullen. They really helped out with the staffing issues, but I still had to be involved. I was the boss, after all.

Rolling to my other side, I punched at my pillow, trying to get back to sleep. My brain just wouldn't stop thinking about work stuff. I groaned, giving up on the idea of getting more sleep. I stretched, swinging my legs over the edge of the bed.

From the other side of the bed, Lulu, my cat, lifted her head.

"Do you want food?"

She yawned, then snuggled into a ball, falling right back to sleep.

Well, sorry to disturb you, ma'am, I thought.

I dropped a scoop of food into her bowl, anyway. It was just my routine. After I was finished in the bathroom, I went downstairs to get some coffee.

Maybe I would make my roommates breakfast, too.

Sawyer, Vee, and I had been friends since middle school. Over twenty years ago, we met and almost instantly clicked. We bonded over the fact we didn't quite fit in any other cliques, so we made our own.

As an adult, I realize now that I had a lot more friends than just the two of them. A few have come to my aide over the last several months in ways I could never repay.

Kyle Rafferty, or, as he is known to most, Officer Rafferty has become someone I see often. He was usually one of the responding officers when there was a crime or murder, like when my sous chef, Earl was killed on opening night for my restaurant.

Oh, Earl, I thought. I missed him daily. He had been a good friend and a great employee.

I have since been involved in three murder investigations. Not something the police wanted me to do, but hey, I was getting better at it. It was also how I had been reunited with many of my old classmates. Well, that and not traveling as much for cooking competitions.

The most recent murder broke my heart when I solved it. The killer had been my childhood babysitter and a good friend of my grandmother's. Granny Ines had been so hurt, she stopped talking to me for a week. We have since talked it out, and she'd explained she wasn't mad at me, more about the situation.

This one with Marco and his friend, Zachary Boyd, would be my fourth, and I did not know where to start yet.

I checked the time. It was still a bit too early to start breakfast. I grabbed my mug of coffee and headed to our office. We had a huge bulletin board that Sawyer's dad built for us. We used it to gather the clues to each murder. It gave us the ability to brainstorm and see everything in one place.

Vee had been disappointed when Detective Richard Upton had told us they don't actually use these boards. Though he said that they'd occasionally use a version to brainstorm, just not like in the movies and TV shows.

I grabbed some blank paper and wrote Zachary Boyd, a homeless veteran, killed in an abandoned building, then pinned that to the board. Next, I wrote Marco's name along with him being the last person seen going into the building, a friend of Zachary's, and the suspect. I tacked his name to the board.

Well, that's all I have so far.

Taking a step back, I stared at the board as a sipped my coffee. I needed more.

My plan for today was to ask him about what the police said to him and what he knew about his friend. He had been so upset the other day about losing him, obviously. I knew he would feel even worse being the last person to see Zachary alive. Not to mention then being arrested as the prime suspect.

Could this guy have been involved in something illegal? It wouldn't be the first time. Plus, I watched the news nearly every day. Weird stuff happens all the time, especially in the larger city of Pinehurst. It was roughly a thirty-minute drive from here. Things could seep over to us.

Many people from our town, who didn't work in the arts, commuted there for work in banking or accounting or whatever other people did. I had been in a kitchen since I was a teen. My grandparents had owned a furniture business in Dashwood, and my Aunt Rita had owned a dance studio. So both small, family-owned businesses that were artistic.

My mother had worked as a teacher until she married Samuel and had my two half-brothers. Samuel did something with computers, but I had almost no relationship with the four of them, so I honestly didn't know.

My two best friends worked at the Dashwood post office and had pretty much since high school. They both got lucky to get on there. Prior to taking jobs there, Vee had worked in a thrift store and been in college. Sawyer worked at a restaurant but hated every minute. Now he was much happier.

One more look at the board before I headed into the kitchen. I started pulling out ingredients for migas. It was something I had grown up eating, but didn't make them often. I chopped up the onion, tomato, and jalapeños. Then I beat the eggs, adding salt and black pepper. Next, I cut tortillas into pieces, adding them to the frying pan to get them crisp. Then I threw in the veggies.

"Hey, good morning," Vee said through a yawn. She headed straight for the coffeepot.

"Hey, I didn't wake you, did I?"

"Of course. I smelled the onions and … oh, are you making migas?" She peeked over my shoulder. "You haven't made those in a while. Yum!"

"Yeah, it just felt like that kinda morning."

I added the eggs to the pan. I watched them bubble, then gently moved them around, ensuring that the eggs and filling mixed, cooking into perfection.

There was a sound upstairs, and then our tall friend came stumbling down into the kitchen. He flashed us a sleepy grin as he grabbed a mug.

"Morning, sunshine," Vee said.

"Morning. Oh, are you making migas?" he asked.

"Yes, I am." I smiled. "You feeling okay?"

"Oh, yeah, just didn't sleep well." He gave a half smile.

I wanted to ask if he had something heavy on his mind as well, but I knew it couldn't have been the same thing. He was likely up playing his newest video game. He had done that before.

"Well, breakfast is ready. Grab a plate." I gestured.

We all piled up the eggs and tortilla mixture, topping it with my homemade salsa that we almost always had on hand. Nobody spoke for a moment, just ate.

My mind kept thinking about my day ahead. Overall, it should be a fairly normal day.

"So, Marco comes back today," I said, breaking the silence. "I'm nervous to see him, but I am also anxious to hear what is going on."

"Do you think he did it?" Vee asked.

That was the million-dollar question.

"I really doubt he would kill someone, especially not someone he had been trying to help." But saying it, I realized maybe I didn't know him well enough to say that. In this case, it was just instinct, my gut, saying that he was a good guy and hadn't done this.

We finished breakfast and my friends got ready for work. It was still a little early for me to head to the restaurant, but I decided to go, anyway.

Might as well get started for the day.

I was nearly done with my morning prep when employees started arriving.

"Morning, Chef."

"Hey, Chef."

"You're early today."

The staff greeted me. I just smiled and said hello and good morning back.

When Marco arrived, his body language spoke volumes. He was normally upbeat, smiling with a positive energy around him. Today he was dragging his feet, had his head bowed, and a frown was plastered on his face.

"Hey, Chef. Thanks for not firing me."

"Why would I fire you?"

"Ya know, the arrest." He looked at me.

"I would never fire you for that. This is a terrible misunderstanding." I was almost sure of that and if I could, I was going to prove it. I just didn't want to get his hopes up.

"Wait? You believe me?"

"I do."

"That means so much to me." He smiled. "Well, I better get to work."

"Before you do, can I just ask you some questions?"

"Oh, yeah, sure."

I took a deep breath. This wasn't an easy conversation and could upset him, but I had to know.

"What happened that night at the building? Why were you there?"

"I often took him food and clean clothes. That night, I had gotten off work, and I took him some of your alphabet soup and cornbread. He loved it."

"Oh, good." I didn't know what else to say, but it felt kind of strange that his last meal was my soup.

"Yeah, I took him food from here a lot. He loved the soup the best." He smiled. "I paid for it, of course."

"No worries if you hadn't. It was a good cause."

He looked at me with tears in his eyes. "You are truly the best. Zach was such a good guy. I just can't believe—" His voice cracked.

I reached out, touching his arm. He smiled weakly at me.

"Did you have more questions, Chef?"

"Yeah, I do."

"Okay, shoot."

"Do you know anyone who would have killed him?"

"I thought about it the last few days, and I can't think of anyone. He was well liked. I would take him to Pinehurst to the VA hospital for meetings or appointments. He was a charming guy. People liked him."

"Okay, so I hate to ask this, but do you think he was doing anything illegal, like selling drugs or maybe even doing drugs? Or part of a gang or something?"

"I mean, anything is possible, I guess, but honestly, no. No, he wouldn't. He was down on his luck, but he wouldn't have done anything shady."

"Alright. Thanks."

He nodded and started to walk away, but then stopped. "Wait, a sec. Are you looking into this? Are you trying to clear my name? Get justice for Zach?"

A slow smile spread across my face as I saw the hope in his.

"I am."

"Oh, wow, that is ... that is amazing. Thank you, Chef." He closed the space between us, wrapping me in a big hug. "I so appreciate you."

"I can't promise anything, but I am happy to try."

With that, we got to work.

Chapter Three

At three o'clock, I turned over my station to June. She was one of my two sous chefs I employed here. I hired her after losing Earl a few month ago.

In my car, I sent a text to Vee and Sawyer, letting them know I was making a stop across town after work. I just wanted someone to know. My plan was to visit the abandoned building on Jamison to see what it looks like.

Even though as a teen, we used to sneak into it to hang out, drink, and just in general cause problems, I had no idea what it looked like today, especially after the fire. When I was a teen, there weren't all the security cameras either. There were some, sure, but mostly inside stores.

S: **Be safe**

V: **Should we meet you there**

Me: **I'm good**

V: **Call if you need us**

I headed across town, smiling as I took in the sights. I loved Dashwood. Having traveled all around the country for cooking competitions, I could really appreciate being at home. Most of the time, life here was simple.

The community has shown such kindness, support, and eagerness to help whenever needed. Many times, I have received assistance and seen how the town backs my restaurant. I'm truly grateful for this community.

I turned up Jamison and immediately saw the burned-up building. I pulled to a stop a block away as the front of the building was blocked.

Stepping out of the car, I looked at the building that faced it.

One camera, two, three cameras. Oh two, no three more. Grand total six.

I made a mental note about the number and locations of them. I walked across the street to get a closer look at the building. The caution tape kept me three feet away from it, but I could see there was a lot of damage.

"Dang." I whistled, taking it all in.

There wasn't much left of it. The roof was gone, collapsed into the center, and piles of brick lay at the base. Through the windows and crumbled walls, I could see steel stuck out in tangled messes and pointing at weird angles. All the surfaces were scarred with scorch marks where the flames licked their way up the walls. I could almost picture their destructive force climbing skyward.

Despite the heat of the day, an icy chill ran up my spine as I took in the full scene. I walked as close as I could. There was still broken glass on the sidewalk, so I couldn't move easily.

A large man with a hard hat came from around the corner. He was marking something on a clipboard and talking into a phone. His eyes cut my way.

"Stan, I need to call you back." He looked me up and down as a smile formed on his face. "May I help you?"

"What happened here?"

"Um," he looked up at the building. "A fire."

His tone was biting with snark. I flashed a mocking smile.

"Yeah, I see that. I just used to live in this area. Grew up right down the road," I gestured. I could see the building my mother and father lived in until I was five. Then my father killed a man, my mother spiraled out of control, and I went to live with my granny and aunt. "I came over to visit a friend and saw it. Shame."

"Ah, well, the entire project here is a mess."

"Yeah, everyone was super excited about the renovations." I looked up at the building. He followed my glance. "It doesn't look like the building can be saved. Do you think it will still happen?"

He eyed me up and down as if trying to decide if he should share. I watched him fight with himself, and his face finally softened, which I took to mean he didn't think I was a threat.

"Yeah, it will probably be a total tear down and rebuild, but the city council will be meeting on Wednesday to decide what will happen with the project."

"Oh, okay. I was planning to attend that meeting. It will be interesting to hear what they say."

His eyes widened as he took a step closer. "Wait. Who are you?"

"Chef Jessica Vasquez. I own The Crock Pot."

"The place with the awesome chicken and dumplings, the alphabet soup, and oh, you had veggie beef the other day?"

I guess we served a lot of soup. I frowned, thinking about the entire menu. We served a much larger menu, including shrimp and grits, chicken fried steaks, and rosemary chicken. Plus, sandwiches, salads, and a wide array of sides and desserts. But I didn't point that out.

Instead, I smiled brightly and proudly.

"Yeah, that's my place."

"Nice. I love your place. I eat there at least twice a week. The cornbread was a great addition. It goes perfectly with your roast chicken or, oh, oh, the sausage and potatoes."

"Thanks. I love to hear that." I grinned. *Oh, good, he had ventured to the rest of the menu, not just soups.*

"So, what is your interest in this building?" He jerked his thumb over his shoulder without taking his eyes off of me. They were dark brown, stormy. I almost never noticed that kind of thing, but they were piercing my soul, making it nearly impossible to ignore their beauty.

My face warmed slightly. I turned as I spoke, hoping he wouldn't notice.

"As I said, I grew up in the area. My friends and I used to sneak in here when we were kids. Now, as a business owner, I was curious about the renovations. It sounded like it would bring in new business to the area."

He rubbed his chin, taking in my words as he looked me up and down. It was unnerving the way he looked at me. Now I was starting to question his association with the building. His phone rang. He checked the display.

"You'll have to excuse me." He walked away from me to take the call. He looked over his shoulder as he spoke. His eyes narrowed as he listened to whoever was on the other side of that call.

"Wait? Who is she?" I heard him say.

Well, bleep!

I decided to leave quickly before he finished his call, as I wasn't sure who he was talking to and what they might say about me. It was already bad that he knew who I was and where I worked.

I walked as fast as I could back to my car, reaching it as I heard him yell out for me. I hopped in, pretending I didn't hear, and took off.

As I turned from Jamison to Lawrence Street, I could see him yelling and running towards me. A nervous giggle escaped as I moved away from the building.

"Oh, my gosh. He knows who I am, but for now, I don't care."

My phone rang, startling me.

"Hey, Vee." I laughed.

"What's so funny?"

"I just ran away from some guy at that building."

"What?" She laughed.

"I was asking him a bunch of questions and then when he took a call, I ran off. He tried to get me to stop, but I didn't." Saying it out loud it didn't actually sound funny. It actually sounded silly.

"Why would you run? You did nothing wrong."

Vee had a point but given what I overheard and the guilt I felt knowing I was really there to spy and look around, I ran. I knew it was a crazy reason, but I was still new at this sleuthing thing, and it made me uncomfortable to snoop around.

"I heard him ask the person something about who I was. I guess I didn't want to find out what they had to say about me."

"Well, that doesn't sound good."

Actually, I chuckled at how ridiculous this all sounded as I said it out loud. I needed to come up with something better to say.

"Trust no one, right?"

"Sure, sure." She laughed.

"But you wanna know the worst part? He knows who I am and where I work, just didn't know why I was asking questions."

"What did you ask him?" Vee asked.

"Just what happened and what the plan for the project was? Nothing crazy."

"That doesn't sound too bad."

"So, what's up?" I got us back on topic.

"Riley asked if we want to go to dinner tonight. She said her treat."

"She wants me to come?"

"Yeah, she said to pay us all back for all the dinners at our place."

"Okay, sounds good." It would be nice to not think about dinner tonight, even if I loved doing it most of the time. A break was always nice. "Where are we going?"

"Undecided, but we are heading to the house now so we can pick something."

"She's with y'all?"

"No, she's gonna meet us shortly, though."

"Okay, I'm heading that way, too. See you soon."

Roughly ten minutes later, I pulled into my spot at our townhouse. I saw Sawyer's car was here, which meant my roommates made it home before me.

Most days I beat them home by an hour, being able to take a shower, get dressed, and start dinner before they ever got home. But since I didn't come straight home, like I usually do, they won today.

"Honey, I'm home!" I bellowed, stepping over the threshold. It was Sawyer's normal greeting, but today I got to do it.

From upstairs, I heard Sawyer's deep laugh and then thundering footsteps coming down the stairs.

"Honey!" He grabbed me, swinging me around. We both laughed.

Vee came from nowhere to join our hugging party. She was barely five feet tall, but she caused us to fall sideways. We fell into a pile of laughter on the floor. I love these two people almost more than anyone.

I didn't know if the three of us would live together forever, but I was going to enjoy these fun moments with my best friends.

"What time will Riley be here?" I asked once we had settled down.

"Should be any minute?"

"Do I have time to take a shower?"

"Of course! We aren't on a schedule." Sawyer smiled.

"Okay, then do I have time to add something to the clue board?"

"Murder board," Vee corrected. That's what Detective Upton had called it.

"Of course, murder board."

"Yeah, what are you adding?" Vee asked.

"I counted the number of cameras facing the building. Six."

"Just facing? What about the back?" Sawyer questioned.

"I didn't get around to the back, so yes, there could be more."

"Why do you think that is relevant?"

"Because if someone else came in after Marco left, we need to see that security footage, right?"

"Oh, I see what you're thinking. Makes sense. Marco wasn't doing anything wrong, so he would have just walked in, but someone else might have tried to sneak in."

"Exactly."

I grabbed a sticky note, added 'six cameras in front', and then stuck it to the board.

"Still not much to go on, but at least we are starting to get a few things."

"Did Marco say anything today? I mean, anything we didn't already know?" Sawyer asked.

"Unfortunately, no. He went to take Zach some food and clean clothes. They visited while Zach ate, then Marco left."

"Someone must have come in after and killed him. Maybe they even saw Marco go in and thought it would be the perfect cover."

"Obviously."

Vee frowned at my blunt reply. I hadn't meant it snarky.

"Sorry, I just meant you're right. Someone saw this as a perfect chance to frame Marco for the murder, but why and who?"

There was a knock at our door.

"Must be Riley." Sawyer quickly strode out of the room.

"Bleep, I need to shower!" I smelled like the restaurant and felt a bit grimy.

Vee chuckled as she left the room. I took one look at the board before following Vee and Sawyer. Sawyer was just opening the door when I joined them. Riley stood up on her tiptoes to greet him with a quick kiss.

"Hey, y'all! I'm glad you were available tonight," Riley said, smiling at us. "Are you ready?"

"Um, no. I still have to shower." I panicked.

"You have time. She has time, right?" Sawyer asked.

"Of course. You're the one I want to thank most for all the delicious food." She looked at Vee and Sawyer. "Y'all understand, right?"

"Yeah, Jess is the chef!"

"We all want to thank her for the great food."

I grinned at the praise. It was just what I do.

"Y'all are so sweet. Okay, give me fifteen minutes." When I reached the stairs, I turned back. "Maybe twenty. It was a busy day."

An hour later, we were sitting at Sushi 73 with various sushi rolls littering the table.

"You have to try this one." Riley said, grabbing a piece with her chopsticks and offering it to Sawyer.

"Oh, wow, that's good. I haven't had that one before."

"Which one was it?" I asked.

"Unagi Avocado Roll."

"Eel, right? That's eel?" Vee asked.

"Yeah, I love eel," Riley said.

"I'm not a huge fan, but I get the appeal." I smiled. "What are y'all doing on Wednesday after work?"

Vee sat up, squealing quietly. "It sounds like we might be going on an adventure."

"Yeah, maybe. Want to go to the city council meeting?"

"Oh, oh! That was fun last time." Vee giggled.

"I'm in!" Sawyer said.

"Oh, shoot. I have second shift on Wednesday," Riley said. "Maybe I can switch with Kayla. She owes me."

I hadn't really wanted Riley along, but I had asked in front of her. She isn't my favorite person. Mostly I tolerate her as my friend's girlfriend.

"Great. Let us know." I forced a smile.

It would be the next step in this investigation.

Chapter Four

Normally, I had Wednesdays off, but June needed today off. Not a problem. We were all flexible with our schedules.

I was working on an order of roast chicken, balsamic glazed salmon, and a chicken fried steak when Ava, one of my servers, came back.

"Hey, Chef, some guy is asking for you."

Her tone caused me to pause and question who it was.

"Customer or a random person?"

"Well, he is sort of a regular customer."

"Sort of?"

"He isn't here to eat today but asked to speak to you."

Bleep! It must be the guy from the construction building.

"Ask if he'd like a drink or if he wants to order something. I'll be out in a minute. Just want to finish this order, then wash up."

"Alrighty." She skipped out.

Once I had the plates out, I passed my station to Hannah. My stomach twisted as I washed my hands. What was he going to say? What would he do to me?

I took a deep breath to steady myself, then plastered on a smile.

Several customers started waving and throwing praise my way.

"Chef, we enjoyed lunch today!"

"Chef, I had the shrimp and grits. Excellent as always."

"I loved the new raspberry jam with the biscuits."

I thanked them all as my eyes searched for the man. Ava caught my eye and pointed behind me to the bar. Turning, he was grinning at me while sipping a peach lemonade. Our bartender today was Ripley. He was the one who came up with the recipe for this lemonade. It was my favorite drink.

I signaled for one, but Ripley already had a glass ready for me.

"Thanks." I turned to the guy. "So, what can I help you with?"

"You ran off the other day before I got to ask you *my* questions." He smirked. "I was very patient answering yours."

"I'd be happy to answer your questions, but first, I have one of my own."

"Alrighty, shoot." He sat back with a cocky smile.

"Who are you?"

"Ah, I guess that's fair, since I know who you are." He wiped his hand on his shirt before offering it to me to shake. "I'm Todd Barber, the Project Manager for the Jamison Heights Complex."

"Oh, you are the project manager for the renovations."

"Yes. That's me and my company."

"How does that work? The city hires you?"

"Not exactly. We are a development company. We come in looking for projects, in this case to revitalize that area, starting with the Jamison Heights building. We then work with the city on zoning and the like to get it done."

"Okay, that make sense."

"Now, let me ask you, why were you snooping around the building?" Before I could speak, he held up a finger. "I want the real reason."

While I thought of how much to share, Ava came over with a bag of food, handing it to Todd. He thanked her, trying to hand her cash. She looked at me. I shook my head.

"Really?" he asked. "Okay, but you deserve a tip," he told her.

"No, no. My boss will take good, *good* care of me." She patted my shoulder before walking off.

"I'm sure you will." He eyed me. "Now, back to my questions. The real reason you were snooping around the building."

I looked around, trying to find Marco. He was busy clearing a table. Todd followed my stare.

"Oh, I understand now. You want to clear your boyfriend's name. Got it."

"He isn't my boyfriend, just an employee."

"Just a busboy. Aren't those a dime a dozen?"

I stared at Todd. *That was rude.*

"No, not at all. He is *an excellent* employee. I can't replace him."

"Sure you can," he said.

I started to stand. "You clearly don't understand."

"No, don't go yet." He shook his head, reaching out to try to stop me. "Sorry, that was rude of me. I really wasn't trying to insult your employee or you. I am sorry. I have more questions."

Okay, fine, I thought. He seemed sincere, but I didn't sit back down. Instead, I stood there staring at him. I took a sip of my drink.

"Quickly, because I do need to get back to work."

"Okay, okay, fair enough, but can we set up a date?" My mouth fell open at his suggestion. He quickly continued. "Not a date-date, but just to talk, over dinner perhaps."

I studied him. He was a handsome man, but not in the movie star, super model way. Tall and broad, with a friendly, almost cocky smile. I bet he played football back in his school days.

I wasn't interested in dating, so that wasn't even a question, but I could do worse. I have definitely, definitely dated worse.

Whoa, slow down, girl. He said it wasn't a date-date. Why do you always do this? A man shows a tiny bit of interest, and you instantly assume it's romantic in nature.

"Fine. Fine."

"Great. I'll call you." He stood, pulling out his phone. "I'll just need your number."

I recited it for him.

"Perfect. I'll call you soon. Oh, and you said you'd be at the city council meeting tonight, right?"

Bleep, he remembered.

"Yep, I plan to be."

"Then I'll see you there." He winked, then walked out.

My face warmed as I watched the door close behind him. What the heck just happened?

"You okay, Chef?" Ripley asked.

"Uh? Oh, yeah." I smiled and made my way back to the kitchen to finish my shift.

An hour or so later, Parker came in to take over as the head chef for the night.

"The roasted chicken has been a hot seller today, for some reason," I told him.

"Because it's good. Plus, Cullen has been advertising it out there on the socials."

"He has?" I should really look at those more, like daily, instead of whenever I remember or when I'm bored.

"Yep. A lot of customers added reviews."

"Oh, that explains it."

I knew he was a solid employee, but Cullen had really gone above and beyond with this social media stuff he was doing. He had taken today off, but I'd have to remember to say something to him when he was back.

Once I was home, I took my time picking an outfit for tonight. Now that I was going to be seeing Todd, I wanted to look extra nice. But here was the problem with my wardrobe: it was either chef's clothing or graphic t-shirts and jeans or yoga pants. There was very little in between.

"I really need to go shopping."

"When? I'm in," Vee said, startling me.

"Ack! When did you get home?"

"Just now. Sorry, I thought you would have heard us."

"No, I guess my closet muted the sounds." I turned to face her. "Where is Sawyer?"

"He was going to call Riley before she starts her shift and then shower."

I nodded, looking through my clothes a bit. "I hate when I have to find a dress up outfit."

"Why do you have to dress up? It's just a city council meeting."

"I know, but last time I did."

"But we both noticed that it wasn't necessary."

That was true, but I had an ulterior motive for wanting to look nice. I just wasn't ready to tell Vee. My face started to warm, so I turned back to my closest.

"I just wanted to look nice, but I didn't want to wear what I did last time."

"There is a guy! Who is it? Spill it." Her voice was firm as she spun me around.

"No guy. Where would I have met a guy?"

"Oh, it's gotta be the guy from the building, right? The one you talked to the other day. The one you ran from!" She laughed.

"How do you always know?" I blew out a laugh.

"I just have a magic power. So, spill."

I filled her in on what happened with Todd from the moment he walked in until he walked out.

"You think he asked you out to get what you know?"

"Possibly." Though I hadn't thought of that.

"Yeah, maybe he heard how good you were at solving these and thought if he stays close to you ..." She stopped.

"Wait, you don't think?"

"Well, I don't want to, but it seems odd, right?"

"Odd that someone might find me attractive?"

"No, of course not. But odd that after just two meetings, he would ask you out."

"I don't even know that he really, truly asked me on that kinda of date. He said just to talk."

"About?"

"Why I was at the building the other day?"

She exhaled.

"So, not a date. Wear what you want? Even if he is interested, he has only seen you twice, right?"

I nodded.

"In your chef's clothes?"

I nodded again.

"If he is interested in you, your clothes won't change that." She smiled brightly. "You good?"

I looked at her. She had a point. It didn't matter. He was either interested in me or not. I shouldn't try to be something I wasn't, and besides, he said it wasn't a date-date.

"Yeah, I know what to wear."

"Glad I could help."

She left, and I hopped in the shower. After, I pulled out a flowy black, ankle-length skirt and a rust red Trash Pandas shirt. Then I grabbed some short ankle boots. Some chunky jewelry would finish the look I was going for. What was the look? Casual, grunge, goth-like? I don't know, but I would be me.

Two hours later, after dinner at Beaks and Brews, we pulled in at city hall. The parking lot was mostly empty.

"This meeting isn't popular, is it?" Vee chuckled.

"There might be a few more cars than last time," I said, trying to be positive, but it didn't look like many in Dashwood cared about how the city worked.

That is why I wanted to get involved and needed to come. I skipped last month's and was here tonight for somewhat selfish reasons. Maybe not selfish but not to understand or better my city.

We walked in to find about half a dozen people waiting in the audience.

"Just like last time," Sawyer whispered.

"The passiveness of the people," Vee whispered.

"We're those people, too," I added.

We took seats in the middle-back. It was quiet, so we sat there silently. As we sat, a familiar face came in, Detective Upton and his wife Brooke. I hadn't seen him in a few weeks. Not since I solved the murder and stolen items in the case at Caruso's Funeral Home.

"Hey, y'all," he said when he saw us.

"Hi, Detective."

"Hey."

"Hi."

"Y'all, remember my wife, Brooke?"

"Of course." I smiled. "Good to see you."

"Good to see you, too. I brought the kids by the restaurant the other day. Aiden loves it."

"Aw, I'm glad."

"He asked for you, but it was your day off."

"Oh, bummer. Maybe next time. I could give him a tour of the kitchen."

"He would love that. He has been playing chef a lot."

"Oh, that sounds cute."

A large figure came into my line of sight. I instantly felt my face warm. All eyes turned to look at the source of my embarrassment. I heard Vee suck in air. Not exactly a gasp, but not a sigh. I didn't want to make eye contact with any of them.

"That's him?" she whispered.

I nodded.

"Okay, I take back everything I said. Date him."

A slow smile formed on my face.

Todd saw me and gave a little head nod as he continued his conversation with the folks he walked in with. I didn't know them. Perhaps they were part of the project team.

Detective Upton leaned over. "Are you here investigating a murder or as a citizen?"

"Both?" I whispered back.

He shook his head at me. "Why are you poking at this?"

"Marco didn't do it."

"You have proof?"

"Do I ever? But I have been right now three times."

"Well, I would say the first one was dumb luck."

"Yes, but if I had the murder board, I think I could have put the clues together."

His mouth fell open, and he just stared at me. Quickly, he composed himself.

"Okay, okay, so what do you have so far?"

I looked around as people were starting to fill the room. It was suddenly quite packed. This didn't seem like the place to talk about this.

"Not much yet, but this might not be the place to talk."

He looked around as if just realizing the room had filled up. "You're right. I'll call you tomorrow. Wait, do you work?"

"Not tomorrow. I filled in for June today."

"Ah, okay, I'll call you tomorrow. Maybe I can drop by to see what you have."

The mayor and city council members filed in. There were whispers among the council members as they saw how many people were in attendance. It was startling. Where had they all come from?

"Protesters," Vee whispered.

Sawyer nodded.

Todd looked over his shoulder, flashing me a wide smile. Was he trying to flirt? The lady to his left turned, shot me a dirty look. When I didn't flinch, she rolled her eyes but turned back around.

The mayor called the meeting to order, reading the summary of last meeting's minutes and then reading today's agenda. Once that was done, she passed to the various districts for status updates and the police department for their updates.

Once all the updates were given, the mayor called for Todd to give an update on the building.

He stood and walked to the microphone.

"Mayor, city council, citizens of Dashwood." He turned to face the audience for a moment. He caught my eye, holding eye contact for just a moment, before turning. "My team and I have inspected the damage to the Jamison Heights building and believe that we can still move forward. However, there is a new budget, and we have to make some changes to the structure now due to the damage. You will find it in the packets in front of you and zoning requirements."

The council members started flipping through the packets. A few made notes, some just read it.

He went through his full plan, but I started to watch the crowd. They were whispering to each other, grimacing at this update or that. It felt like the room was filled with static electricity, and like a powder keg ready to blow, one spark was going to set it off.

It happened when the council opened the floor for comments.

Shouts of ban the building, not in my town, and give us a park filled the air. Detective Upton held on to his wife's hand as the crowd surged forward. He looked over at us, giving us a quick nod to move toward the exit. We followed his lead.

Suddenly, I saw six police officers standing near the front of the room. I don't even know where they came from. They stood there trying to keep the crowd back.

"I think we should get out of here before things get crazier," Sawyer said.

"I want to see what happens," Vee giggled.

"It is just pure chaos." I searched the crowd of protesters for Todd. He was standing in front of the mayor and a few other ladies, trying to keep the chaos away from them as the officers tried to get people out of the room.

"Can Brooke go with y'all? I want to help get this under control, but I want her safe." Detective Upton looked at us.

"Absolutely," Sawyer said.

I guess that settled it; we were leaving. I looked again for Todd. He and the city council members were going out a side door. I guess they would be okay.

The yelling got louder as the police continued to order the crowd out, so we made a run for our car.

Brooke gave us directions to their house. Sawyer followed them, and soon we pulled up at a dark-colored craftsman house with a low-pitched roof and wrap-around porch.

It was located on the far west side of town. It was nearly outside of Dashwood limits. It had a white picket fence around it and random toys were littering the yard. I thought of the cute little boy who they belonged to.

"Thank you all so much for the ride. Things got crazy, huh?" Brooke said.

"Yeah, that was crazy."

"Is it always like that?" she asked.

"We have only been to one other, and it wasn't like that."

"Well, it was … interesting." She laughed.

"Tell Aiden hi from me," I said.

"And me!" Vee added. "I hope he still has my Freddy bear."

"Oh, he does. Carries it everywhere. We left it at the park, and he had a meltdown. Rich had to run out at nearly nine at night to find it."

"Oh, dear. Glad he found it." Vee smiled.

With the goodbyes said, she hopped out. We watched her go into the house before we also drove off.

"I guess I'll be adding protesters to the board when we get home."

"Yeah, definitely."

"That was crazy."

"Why do you think they are so … so, um, passionate over a park? That seemed excessive," I said.

"People like their causes." Vee shrugged.

"Yeah, just watch the national news. People are out there raging over the craziest things." Sawyer laughed.

It was true. I could see the point of not having a building with more businesses that would bring more traffic, more people, and likely change the small town feel of our town. But as a business owner, I liked the idea of more development.

Was I that passionate about anything? I mean, I did love cooking, but to protest? To form a mob and swarm a room? No, there was nothing I could think of that I would get that insanely crazed about.

Chapter Five

My roommates had just left for work, and I was cleaning up after breakfast. They had requested migas again. I didn't mind. I loved them, too.

I had no real plans for my day off, but I was waiting to hear from Detective Upton. He wanted to come by today to see what we currently had saved on our clue board. I had warned him it wasn't much yet. He said he was okay with that, and we could compare notes.

Todd messaged me last night to see how I was feeling after the frenzied meeting.

T: **You make it out, okay?**

Me: **Yeah. You?**

T: **Barely. I thought my number was up.**

He included a winky face, so I knew he meant it as a joke.

Me: **I bet!**

T: **We need to finish our conversation. When are you free?**

My heart stopped beating for a second. It was a ridiculous response. I barely knew him and my impression had been a negative one, so then why was my reaction to crush on him? Plus, he had not shown any romantic interest in me, so why were my brain and heart acting like this?

Me: **Not until next Wednesday.**

Okay, I lied, but that was fine. I wasn't ready to see him.

T: **I thought you worked during the day, you can't go to dinner with me one night?**

I inhaled a slight laugh. He was smooth, or at least he was trying to be.

Me: **I could do a dinner. Just not Sunday.**

T: **Do y'all do family dinners, too?**

Me: **We do**

T: **That's the best, right? Okay, how about Friday night?**

Me: **Yeah, Friday works.**

T: **Okay, I can pick you up at 5:30**

Me: **Sounds good.**

I followed that with my address. My finger hovered over the send button for a second. Maybe I should meet him at the restaurant. No, it should be fine. I hit send.

He replied almost immediately.

T: **Great. See you then.**

Me: **See ya then.**

I reread the entire texting chain after we said goodbye. Butterflies flitted in my stomach.

Thinking about it now, I thought perhaps I should go shopping. Maybe Auntie Rita and Granny Ines would like to go with me. I just wish I knew what time the detective thought he would be here.

After I finished the dishes, I headed to the office to look at what I had on the board. Last night, I added the protesters, but I wasn't sure exactly where to put them. I simply added them to one side with a question mark.

In reading their signs and listening to their chants, it sounded like they wanted the park that was originally proposed. I couldn't blame them. A nice park would be a welcome sight in that part of town. We had a number of nice parks closer to downtown and over on the west side, near where the Upton family lived.

But could one of them have gotten overzealous and killed Zach?

My phone chimed. It was Detective Upton asking if I was available.

Me: **Yes**

U: **Okay, on my way**

Well, that was good. I wouldn't have to wait all day, and he shouldn't stay long. I could still go shopping. I would text Auntie Rita and Granny Ines to ask if they wanted to go with me, but first, I headed to the kitchen to start a fresh pot of coffee, just in case he wanted anything.

I shot off a text asking about shopping and lunch. Granny replied quickly with a yes, followed quickly by Auntie Rita's yes.

Me: **Great. I'll come over around 10**

GI: **Sounds perfect, Mija**

And now I wait. I sat at our kitchen island, listening to the drip of the coffee. It was a special blend that was created by a local coffeehouse. It was a smooth, rich roast. Sawyer and I loved it black. No sugar, no creamer or milk needed. Vee, on the other hand, liked it lighter with a hazelnut creamer that the same coffeehouse created.

There was a knock at the door. I hopped up to answer it.

"Hey, Detective Upton. Come in."

"Thanks. Good morning." He smelled the air. "Coffee?"

"Yes, I made it for you."

"You're awesome. I didn't get to have any yet."

"How do you take it?"

"Is it from Malory's?" he asked without answering.

"Of course."

Everyone loved Malory's coffee. It had a unique smell to it. Almost like cinnamon and bitter coffee, but in the best way. Her place was called Roasted Beans and almost always had a line wrapped around the building. We ordered it for the restaurant, so I rarely had to go to the actual shop.

"Black."

"Coming up." I grabbed him a mug and filled it.

"Thank you. Can I see the board?"

"Of course."

We walked back to the office. He took a long drink from the mug as he looked at the board.

"Not much," he finally said.

"Yeah, but it hasn't been a full week yet." I frowned.

I knew it wasn't much, but it was all I had so far. He knew how this worked. I bet he didn't even have this much yet, well, except maybe some forensic details like autopsy and maybe an idea of how the fire started. Was it intentional or accidental? Was the fire meant to cover up the murder?

I gasped and looked at him.

"What?" he asked.

"Was the fire set to cover up the murder?"

"Yeah, we believe it was."

"But why this homeless guy? It wasn't like he was a harm to anyone."

"That's what makes Marco Reyes the perfect suspect."

I stared at him, mouth agape. "Someone *did* frame him."

"That's what I think, but I have no real proof yet, so I'm hoping your natural curiosity and willingness to help others will work in my favor." He winked.

"So, you aren't going to tell me to stop?"

"I have tried before, but you and I both know you're not going to listen to me at all. I'm going to lean in this time. You have this." He waved to the board. "The Chief frowns on these. He says we should be able to do our job without TV props. While I agree to a point, we also don't have all the resources of a larger city."

"Does that matter?"

"Yes, it matters. Our forensic team is one person and one intern. They are months behind. I am the only detective, and we have a dozen other officers. We can't be everywhere and investigate everything the way I would like. It's frustrating."

"Why not go to a larger city?"

"Brooke's family is here. She wants the kids to grow up how she did with family dinners, holidays surrounded by cousins, and the slower paced life of Dashwood."

"That makes sense."

Though I had cousins and siblings, it wasn't always the fairytale family relationship you saw on television. I did, however, enjoy family dinners with my Granny, Auntie Rita, and my friends.

"Alright, let's add blunt force trauma." He grabbed a paper, wrote it, then tacked it to the board.

"Were there … what's it called?" I snapped my fingers repeatedly, trying to recall the word. "Oh, yes, an accelerator used for the fire."

He whipped his head to look at me.

"What?" I said innocently. "I know stuff."

He chuckled softly. "Yes, there was."

"I looked at the building and I could see some of the marks looked to be more charred. It was almost a splashing pattern, as if someone had poured stuff and it splashed. Plus, I thought that maybe it got hotter in those places where the accelerant was added."

"Very good. Okay, so let's put that down, too."

He added it. Then added the word 'FRAMED.'

I had a chill of validation run through my body. That was exactly what I thought from the moment I watched Officers Rafferty and Perez load Marco into their car.

"Thank you," I said, my voice cracking.

His eyes widened just slightly, and had I not been looking right at him, I would have missed it.

"You really care about your employees."

"I really do."

"I had always heard that working in a kitchen was … well, hell. I have seen some of those reality shows with the chefs screaming and cursing their employees."

"Yeah, been there, and I vowed I wouldn't be like that. I do lose my temper some, but not like you see on television."

"I guess, just like police dramas, you can't believe everything you see."

"Truth."

"Well, that's all I wanted." He downed the coffee, handing me the cup. "Thank you for the cup of joe and the information."

I walked him out. That was easy. Not a lot of new information exactly, but it was something. I walked back to the office to take one more look, then headed upstairs to shower before going to pick up my grandmother and aunt for shopping and lunch.

Chapter Six

"This outfit is so perfect for you," Vee said, as I modeled it for her. "Where are you going?"

"He said Mills Steakhouse." I felt a slight warmth rise up my neck to my cheeks. I touched them, expecting them to be burning hot. They weren't, at least to the touch.

"That's a date place," Vee blurted.

"It can be a business meeting place, too." Not sure why I was trying to justify this. Who cares if it was a date or a business meeting? I was single, and I was a business owner. Both things fit.

"Yeah, but this is a date outfit." She winked.

"Wow, look at you!" Sawyer whistled as he came in.

"You look great," Riley added, coming up from behind him.

"Thanks." I smiled.

I turned back to my full-length mirror to look at myself. Granny had been the one to pick out the black maxi dress. It was a floral pattern, but it wasn't exactly flowery. It was almost a goth or grunge like style.

"This is exactly you. Not super girly girl, but still feminine," Granny Ines had said.

"And it fits your frame well," Auntie Rita added.

They suggested simple silver accessories that I would never have picked normally, but somehow it all worked. Even the silvery gladiator sandals.

"Do you think it was the best idea to meet him here? Shouldn't you have met him at the restaurant instead? Safer," Riley asked.

We all turned to look at her. Why would she say that? Not that I hadn't thought about it once or twice, but I think it was just nerves. My last date had ended up with a murder.

"I thought about it, but I ... I just decided it would be okay," I stammered.

Sawyer elbowed her.

"What? We were all thinking it."

"Thinking what?" Vee asked.

Riley exhaled as she rolled her eyes.

"What if he is the killer? He could be trying to get close to you."

Vee and I looked at each other. Not sure what she was thinking, but I was trying to find an argument to give. I couldn't. Vee had already suggested that Todd might be using a date to get close to me to learn about the investigation. This was a worse reason than that.

Bleepity-bleep, Riley. Why are you here? I thought.

She always gave voice to my fears. I did not like that.

Honestly, she had a point. The day I had gone to the abandoned building site, he had seemed angry as I drove away. Not that I talked to him, just his stance as I caught him in the rearview mirror. Hands on hips, legs wide, and a reddened face. At the time, it made me giggle out loud, but now I was wondering if I had misread it.

"I think it will be fine." I said it as much to convince myself as I was saying it to them.

"Well, you would know." Riley tried to smile, but it was more of a grimace.

The doorbell camera chimed on all of our phones just as a knock on the door echoed up the stairs.

"That must be him." I smoothed my hair before smiling at my friends. They followed me downstairs to check out the guy.

Holding the handle, I turned to my friends. Sawyer and Vee gave me a thumbs up with huge smiles. Riley stood there, arms crossed. *That's the confidence boost I needed right before opening the door. Thanks, guys.* I grinned back at them.

He knocked again, so I took one deep breath before swinging the door open.

"Hi, sorry. I was upstairs," I said.

"Hi, well, it was worth the wait. You look beautiful."

Beautiful? I had never been called beautiful before. I looked down at myself, then back up.

"Thanks, so do you. Well, not beautiful, but you know, handsome," I stammered. I heard Riley trying to hide a laugh. I fought the urge to turn around and snap at her.

"Thank you." He flashed a grin, showing his deep dimples that I had only just noticed. How had I not noticed?

"By the way, these are my roommates and best friends, Vee and Sawyer. And this is Riley, Sawyer's girlfriend."

He looked behind me.

"Nice to meet you, folks. I'll have her back by curfew."

We all laughed. It was a nice icebreaker.

He held out his arm like a hook. "Ready?"

"Um, yes," I said, looking over at my friends.

Vee thrust my purse my way. It was a smaller purse than I normally carried, but she talked me into it. My usual bag of choice was an oversized hobo style. This was a three by five-inch cross-body purse. I could carry a small, credit card sized wallet, my cell phone, and keys. That was about it.

I hooked my arm with his and took the couple of steps down from our foyer to the sidewalk. He pointed towards his SUV parked across the street and a few doors down. The unit he was parked in front of had recently been vacated.

Though it was empty, there was a light on inside. It caught my eye, distracting me from something he said.

"Jess?" His voice broke the spell of staring at the light. "You okay?"

"What? Oh, yeah, I just … thought I saw something." I shrugged, climbing into the car, flashing him a smile as he held the door open for me. "Thank you."

"Of course."

He shut it and while he walked around to the driver's side, I looked up at the vacant unit. Why did I have that creepy feeling like I was being watched? No, it was probably that old couple in the unit next to it. She was always watching the comings and goings on the street.

He settled in and started down the road.

"Alrighty, now that you can't run away, and we can't be interrupted, let's chat about why you're interest in this building."

He went right for it. No surprise really, but yikes, there was no getting out of this. I shifted, clearing my throat.

"Yeah, um." What to say? What to say? I guess honesty is the best policy. "As you know, my employee was arrested for the murder of that man, Zachary, and I just don't buy it."

"Why not?"

"He doesn't have the personality for it."

"Anyone can have the personality for it." He chuckled, giving me a wink.

I think his comment was meant to tease, but it sent a chill through me. Riley's words sounded in my head. *"What if he is the killer?"*

Instead of arguing or jumping from the moving car, I laughed lightly.

"I don't." I honestly didn't think I could kill anyone, except maybe if they hurt Lulu. The time someone broke in and I couldn't find her, I really wanted to hurt someone.

"Good to know," he said. "I don't either, but you might be surprised."

Thankfully, we pulled into the crowded and very public parking lot. It felt safe to be near other people, just in case this eerie feeling I was suddenly feeling came true.

"Hold on," he said before I could hop out.

I watched as he ran around the car to open my door. It was not something I was used to by anyone. My stomach fluttered at the gesture. Do killers do that? I thought of the many serial killer docuseries I'd watched. The killer was always the charming guy. I shrugged and figured we were in a public place, at least.

Plus, I really wanted to give him the benefit of the doubt on this, so I was going to act as normal as possible.

"Oh, thank you."

"My mama taught me well." He then offered his bent arm.

"Give her my compliments on a job well done."

He grinned as I slipped my arm through his. He guided me into the restaurant as if I was the queen of the world or something. It felt weird and good at the same time.

Being this close to him, I felt short and smaller than I had in years. Most of my life, I was the same size or larger than my dates. He wasn't much larger than me. It was more the confidence and energy he had about him that made him seem bigger than his six foot four-inch frame presented.

Wow, this really felt like a date-date.

He gave his name to the hostess, Steph. She looked at me with a wide smile.

"Hey, Chef!"

"Hey, Steph. How are you?"

"Living the dream! Do you want me to tell Jen that you are here?"

Jen was the executive chef at Mills Steakhouse, and we had gone to culinary school together. Our career paths took very different paths after. I went on to mostly do cooking competitions, working in kitchens to keep my skills up, and pay my bills. She worked her way up the ladder here at Mills from dishwasher to executive chef, over the course of her twenty plus working years.

"No, no. Don't bother her."

"I'm going to tell her, anyway. She'll want to know." Steph gave a laugh.

"Well, I can't stop you," I joked.

Todd looked back and forth, following our brief conversation.

"Oh, sorry, I should get you seated." She looked back at her list. "Let me see. We had you … here, but I am going to move you … no, wait … ah, this one. Best table in the house." Her head popped up, a proud grin on her face. "Follow me."

We walked through the dining room to a table at the far side, almost private, but with a good view of the restaurant.

"Steven will be your server and will be over in a sec. Enjoy, and as always, good to see you, Chef."

I watched as she darted straight into the kitchen. Knowing how busy Mills always was, I hated bothering Jen. She would likely be swamped back there.

"Wow, I feel like I'm with a celebrity," Todd teased once we were alone.

"Nah, not me." I laughed. "But the chefs in the area, especially the head or executive chefs, all know each other."

"I thought it was a competitive field."

"Oh, it can be for sure. Not everyone gets along, especially in some of the larger cities. However, most of us here in Dashwood are friends and have known each other since before we got to this level."

"Makes sense."

"Hello. Welcome to Mills. I'll be your server. Steven." He fidgeted a bit. "Do you want to hear our specials?"

"Sure," Todd said.

Steven gave a rundown of the various special dishes for the night.

"And I highly recommend the grilled ribeye with garlic blue cheese mustard sauce with scalloped potatoes and wedge salad. It is excellent."

"I second that." A sweaty, but smiling Jen came to stand by the table.

"Hey, Jen." I stood to hug her.

Even though I wasn't a hugger with everyone, she was someone who I felt a special connection with. We had both ended up in Mr. Duncan Jones's culinary arts program for almost the same reason. We had been troublemakers. We met for the first time in his class and had been paired to work on a project together.

"Hey, yourself. You look great!"

"So do you."

"Thank you. Well, I can't stay but wanted to say hi. Get an appetizer or dessert on me," she said, looking at Steven so he understood not to charge us.

"I can't do that."

"No, you absolutely can. You comped my entire meal last time I was over at your place."

"I just had to make sure you understood who you were competing with."

"Ha, no competition." She gestured around at the gorgeous, high-end restaurant. "I am truly winning."

We shared a laugh as I took a seat and she returned to the kitchen. Steven took our drink order and then left us to look over the menu.

Todd glanced at the menu, but then I could feel him staring at me.

"What?" I looked up.

"Who *are* you?"

"I'm nobody. Just a chef with a lot of friends in the industry."

"I can see that, but wow, I was already interested in you ... but wow." He picked up his menu again. "As a professional, do you have any recommendations?"

"I think the special he mentioned, the ribeye, would be good. That's probably what I'm getting."

"Then I will too, even though I'm not totally sure what it is. Do you want an appetizer?"

"The crab cakes are excellent. The fried asparagus is, too. That's what I normally get."

"Awesome. I like both of those."

Steven brought the drinks, took our order, then left us alone once again.

"Okay, so now that we have established that neither of us has murderous thoughts, what had you hoped to find at the building that day?"

"Like I told you, I lived in the area and used to hang out in it with my friends. We would run all through it exploring and causing trouble."

"So that wasn't a lie?"

"No, that was true. The only part I kinda lied about was that I was there to look around, or at least as much as I was able to. Obviously, not much, since it is extremely dangerous."

"Okay, but what do you want to know?"

"Who did it? Obviously."

"And you thought you could see that just by creeping around a burned-out building?" He chuckled. His laugh was deep and smooth. My stomach flip-flopped.

"Yes, but not exactly. I thought there might be clues or something."

"Well, I can tell you what I know."

"You would?"

"Yes, you just had to ask me." His smile brightened and his eyes twinkled.

"I didn't think anyone would help me."

"You just assumed I was a bad guy."

"No, not at all."

"Then why did you speed off when I wanted to talk with you? And why did I have to practically corner you to get you to go out to dinner with me?"

"I didn't speed off." Even though I actually had, but didn't want to admit it. "I just had to be somewhere."

"Uh-huh, yep, I believe you. Totally."

I snickered. I never snickered, but what other reaction did one have when they were actively being flirted with? Wait, was he flirting? It had been so long that I forgot what actual flirting was.

"I did. I had just gotten off work and needed to get home."

"For a delivery? A service provider? A boyfriend? Family?"

"Why do you care?" I asked coyly.

"Maybe I'm interested." He smiled.

"Interested in what?"

He threw his head back as he laughed at me. A tear rolled from his eyes. I didn't think it was that funny. It was an innocent question.

He finally composed himself, looking right in my eye. "Interested in you."

"Me?"

"Yes. You're interesting, attractive, ambitious, courageous. All things I admire."

I stared at him. I guess I had hoped that would be his answer, but it still surprised me.

"Oh."

Thankfully, our server brought our food, so we were once again interrupted.

"Some day, I am going to learn to have important conversations with you in private." Todd added with a wink, as we both cut into our steaks.

We never did get back on the topic of the murder or building fire, at least not while we were at Mills Steakhouse. We talked about all the other first date topics, like favorite movies, music, childhood stuff, but not murder.

An hour later, he settled the bill, and we headed out. In his car, he turned to me.

"Do you mind if I stop by City Hall? I forgot some documents there that I need to review before tomorrow."

I hesitated only a moment, going through the pros and cons of being alone with him in an empty building. They had security cameras and likely a security guard on duty, so it was probably safe.

I don't know why I was still fighting myself with this, but these murder investigations caused me to be more paranoid about people. I really wanted to not have these thoughts.

"Yeah, not a problem."

"Great! You get to see my work side, like I got to see yours." He gestured to the restaurant before putting it in reverse.

Minutes later, we were pulling in. He parked in a spot labeled with his name.

"See? I am big stuff, too." He chuckled.

"Nice." I laughed along.

I followed him to the second floor and then to an office with his name on the door.

"Here we are. My kingdom." He pushed the door open.

It was extremely neat inside. I'd pictured piles of disheveled papers, post-it notes, and boxes overflowing with cylinders of blueprints and whatnot.

He had one of those clacky ball things. Newton's cradle, I think, is the name. Then on the other side was sandscape art. I used to love those things. Mr. Jones had one on his desk for years. I would go in there and flip it to watch the sand fall.

There were general office supplies, a desk phone, and a monitor, but those were the only other things on the desk. He had a nice view out the window.

"Is that the rose garden?" I asked, pointing.

"It is." He walked to stand next to me at the window. "I had fun, even if we still didn't get to talk more about the reason for all this."

"Yes, I had fun, too."

He reached over, gently touching my hand. "I'd like to see you again, as long as you don't think I'm a killer."

Did I want to date him? Was he a killer? I studied him for a moment. *Yet to be determined.*

"I'd like that, and no, I don't think you're a killer." I laughed quietly. I guess my inner voice and my outer voice did not agree. Either way, I had just agreed to a second date with someone who could be a suspect.

"Well, I got what I came for." He grabbed the folder off the desk. "Ready to go?"

I took a final look around at his minimalist office.

"Yep."

We walked hand-in-hand out of the building, and then he drove me home. He parked across the street from my house, in front of the empty unit.

He turned towards me with a smile. "I'll walk you to your door."

At the door, we stood there for a moment. This part was always awkward. Here we were adults but standing at the door like unsure teenagers.

He broke the silence first.

"Well, I had a good night. Talk later."

He leaned over, as if he was going to kiss me. My mind and lips prepared for it, but he landed the kiss on my forehead. Honestly, it was almost more romantic and intimate than a kiss on the lips.

Whoa. I thought as the contact ended. He grinned and then walked back to his car. He didn't drive off immediately, so I ducked into the house quickly.

I went to peek through the blinds, catching the moment he drove away, sighing slightly at my silliness. This man was not interested in me, right?

There was a sound behind me. I turned slowly to find Vee standing there with a huge smirky grin on her face.

"Did you have a nice time?"

"Um, yes." I sighed.

"Ohmygosh! You're smitten with him."

"He asked me on a second date, and he kissed me, well, on the forehead, but still."

"Okay, okay, but the more important question, did he do it?" She meant had he killed Zachary Boyd, then framed Marco.

I started to answer, but then slammed my mouth shut.

"I don't know," I finally said. "We kept getting interrupted and only talked briefly about it."

"Well, maybe on the second date," she said with a laugh, turning to head upstairs.

I glanced once more out the window, but his car was long gone. Movement in the empty unit across from us caught my eye. It almost looked like two people standing at the window looking out. I did a double take, but there was nothing there.

Chapter Seven

I checked the clock for the hundredth time this afternoon. I was running late getting out of here; we needed to be at Granny Ines's in forty minutes for Sunday dinner, and here I was still at work.

My mom, stepfather, and half-brothers were supposed to be there today. We had an extremely dysfunctional relationship, so I didn't want to add any more fuel to that fire by being late and giving any of them reason to chastise me. My brothers, Christopher and Bryan, were relentless when it came to picking on me.

My mom was more of the passive aggressive type.

"Order up!" I yelled for a runner or even a busser, server, someone.

We were short staffed today, and it was crazy busy, which is why I was running so late. Even with Parker here to take over my station, neither of us could keep up. I don't know where all the people came from.

It was great for the bottom line, and I'm not really complaining, but wow, I was tired. This crowd was also stoking my ego as they were coming to eat my food. It was the dream.

I also knew Granny would understand the lateness. Hard work was something she respected.

Finally, I was able to get to a point where I could turn over the station fully to Parker. I grabbed my stuff and practically ran out the back door, right into the rain.

"Ahh!" I squealed as I ran to my car. Now I was soaking wet, but at least I was heading home first. I could shower before heading to Granny's.

But the second problem which would slow me even more was nobody in Dashwood would drive fast, especially in the rain. Dashwood was a small town, so people were never in a hurry. When you added a change to the weather, it would cause them to go at a snail's pace. I still loved it here.

Before pulling out of the parking lot, I hit the phone button on my car's display to call Granny.

"Hello?" Her familiar voice filled my car.

"Hi, Granny. It's Jessie."

"Oh, Mija! Are you on your way?"

"Actually, we are going to be a little late. Things at the restaurant were a bit crazy today. With the rain, people were staying longer, and we were short-staffed. You know, all the things." I laughed.

"Part of owning a business. Do you know how late you'll be?"

"Maybe twenty minutes later than usual."

"Okay, that's fine. We have you kids coming and Edie is here. She'll be joining us, but nobody else is coming."

"Oh, I thought my mom and them were coming." I wanted to breathe a sigh of relief but held it until I heard what she had to say.

"She called earlier. Christopher has to work, and Bryan has a headache or something." She sighed. "I don't know if that's true, but they aren't coming."

Sounds like a bunch of excuses, but I let out my sigh just the same. Perhaps they had been dreading this dinner as much as I had been.

"Okay, well, we will be there as soon as I can get home and changed."

"We will see you soon, then. Love you."

"I love you, too."

Minutes later, I pulled in front of our townhouse. There was a moving van in front of the empty unit. I didn't see anyone moving anything or anyone at all. I guess the rain made it difficult and it was not ideal to unload everything. At least it confirmed that I wasn't crazy. There had been movement in the windows.

"Honey, I'm home!" I yelled.

"Yay! We can finally leave. I'm so hungry," Sawyer said, coming to greet me.

"Did you see the new neighbors?"

They rushed to the window, looking out.

"When did that show up?" Sawyer looked down at Vee.

"I didn't see anything or anyone," she said.

"I guess the weather hasn't made moving easy."

"I guess, but weird that nobody mentioned anything." Sawyer pouted.

"Who?" Vee and I asked at the same time.

"Barb and Sandy."

They were the ladies in 1408 that he sometimes had hot tea and conversation with.

"Would they know?"

"Lamar is Barb's son and Sandy's nephew."

Lamar was our landlord. He owned the dozen units on our block.

"Oh, I didn't know that."

"They know everything. I guess I need to have tea with them tomorrow." He rubbed his hands together as he let out an evil laugh. "I'll get all the gossip."

"Good plan," I said. "Well, let me go get ready. Give me fifteen. No, make it twenty."

Nineteen minutes later, I came downstairs fresh and ready to go. Thankfully, the rain had slowed quite a bit, so we didn't have to worry about getting wet.

"For once, it's not me holding us up," Vee pointed out with a laugh as we made our way to the car.

"Gee thanks, but yeah…" I laughed.

Sawyer drove us over to Granny's. We sang all the way over. I loved time with my friends. It was easy to be with them. I could be myself and not think.

We pulled up at the curb. I saw Ms. Edie's car in the driveway behind Auntie Rita's.

"Oh, is Edie here?" Sawyer asked.

"She is. I forgot to tell y'all."

"I love her," he said, climbing out of the car.

Of course he did. He loved everyone and Edie was good people. She was one of my aunt's dearest friends. They had been friends for years.

"There you kids are," Granny Ines said, stepping out onto the porch. "I hope y'all are hungry."

"Starving," Sawyer said, hugging her. "What are we having?"

"You!" She laughed, squeezing his arm. "I made all your favorites. Tacos and enchiladas with rice and beans."

"You know me so well, Ms. Ines. Those are my favorites."

"Mine too!" Vee yelled.

"All my favorites," I added.

We stepped into the house and were immediately hit with the wonderful smells of home. It was comfort, security, and love.

"There are my favorite kids." Auntie Rita danced into the living room with Ms. Edie right behind her. "We weren't sure you were going to make it."

"Yes, sorry. Work was crazy today, and we were short staffed."

"Ah, well, it happens," Auntie Rita said. "How is Marco doing?"

"Marco?" Her question caught me off guard. How did she know Marco? I knew she'd been to the restaurant. Maybe she'd gotten to know him there.

"Marco Reyes. His mom, wife and his daughter all go to our church."

"Oh, yes, Marta Reyes is the sweetest lady," Edie said.

"I didn't know that. Do you know them well?"

"Marta is in our Bible study group. You've met her," Auntie Rita said.

"I have?" I couldn't picture her at all.

"Yeah, yeah. Here." She pulled out her phone, flipping through some of the pictures until she found the one she was looking for. "She's the one in brown with white polka dots."

I looked at the pictures, looking for the lady in brown with white polka dots. My eyes found her. She was a small woman with a neat bob haircut. She had a grandmother look about her that was sweet, but honestly, my only thought was, how did Marco come from this tiny woman?

I tried not to laugh at the thought.

"Okay, I have met her. I didn't realize she was Marco's mother."

"She has been extremely upset, obviously, with his arrest," Edie said.

"She missed our group lunch yesterday," Auntie Rita said.

"Yes, she did. Poor thing." Edie frowned.

"She said that he isn't doing well, either. He and his sweet wife have been fighting. Selene is threatening to leave him, but Marta has talked her into staying. That's why she wasn't there. It has been taking a toll on that whole family," Auntie Rita added.

I could imagine. I remember how my father's arrest had torn our family apart. Being only five years old at the time, I am sure there were even more complex things I hadn't seen. As an adult, I could see Marco's decline.

"Are you doing anything about this?" Granny asked me. Her tone had me wanting to confess everything I had ever done wrong.

"I … I am investigating it. Of course, I am."

"Okay, good, good. You figured out what Lolly had been up to all those years, so I am sure you can figure out who really killed that poor man." Granny patted her lap. "Welp, are you all ready to eat?"

I guess she felt we had the business talk out of the way. Granny's word was always final. We moved to the dining room.

"Do you need help with the food?" Sawyer offered.

"I'd love your help." Granny smiled at him. "I'll show you what to bring in."

"I'll help too." Vee followed them into the kitchen.

A moment later, the three came back in carrying platters of food. With that, all talk was kept casual. No more talk of murder or Marco. I was thankful. I really didn't want to think about it for a few hours.

After dinner was eaten, and everything cleaned up, we pulled out cards to play a few hands. It was a fun night of good food, good company, and laughs.

When we left, Granny loaded us down with tons of leftovers.

"I know how much you love this," she said to Sawyer. "I gotta take care of my favorite kids."

"Thank you, Ms. Ines. We love you."

"I love you, too." She kissed his cheek, then turned to me. "Now, you work hard to find this killer, okay?"

It was less of a question than a demand, but I smiled and agreed. The rain had started up again, so once the goodbyes were done, we darted from the porch to the car. I looked back at my grandmother and aunt standing there, waving. I waved as we drove away.

"Wow, she's really putting the pressure on you," Vee said.

"Yeah, right? I am sure I can figure this out, but how?" I mumbled.

We drove home in mostly silence. The rain was blinding, but we made it home without incident. We settled into our evening routine. Sawyer playing games and Vee and I playing on our phones. Lulu joined us on the couch.

As I was going to bed, I got a text from Todd. For the next hour, we messaged back and forth. It was fun and exciting getting to know him. He wasn't into art the same way Colt had been, especially Neal Barney, who was my favorite local artist.

T: **I don't get him. It is just mythical creatures in flowers.**

Me: **But it is fun**

T: **Is it? (smiley face)**

Me: **YES**

T: **Not my thing, but I guess I can see the appeal**

Me: **Well, who do you like?**

T: **Local?**

Me: **Yes**

T: **I can't remember her name, but she does those landscapes**

Me: **Tilly Martin**

T: **Yes, Tilly Martin. I like the real feeling of the watercolors, especially how she captures the sky.**

Me: **I have a few of hers at my restaurant.**

T: **That's where I saw them first. Then at the last art festival, I bought one.**

Me: **Nice**

T: **Anything new with the investigation?**

That was a whiplash like subject change. Where had that come from?

Me: **No, nothing.**

T: **You know, there are no cameras facing the back of the building.**

Me: **Oh.**

I didn't know what else to say.

T: **Have you heard the Trash Pandas are going to do a show in a few weeks?**

Whiplash topic change again. I guess since I didn't say much about the building, he figured time to move the conversation forward. We kept talking about music, art, and food for another hour. He never brought up the building or murder again, and I didn't have anything to share on it, so it just dropped.

I laid there thinking about what he said. It led to one of those tossing and turning nights. In the morning, I knew that I would have to go look for myself.

Had he said it to bait me into going? Tease my curiosity? Whatever his reason for bringing it up, it definitely stirred my interest in returning to the building.

It would have to wait until after work though.

Chapter Eight

It had rained all day yesterday and most of today, but I was going to run over to Heroes and Villains Comics. The owner, Monte, had sent out his monthly newsletter and mentioned new artwork. I wanted to check it out.

I looked down at my outfit. Oh well, Monte had seen me in my chef's clothes before, so who cares?

I messaged Vee and Sawyer, but they wouldn't be off early enough to go with me today. There weren't any new Pop Funko figurines for Vee to check out and none of the comics Sawyer usually reads. So, this was just going to be a quick trip for me.

I clocked out and made my way across town. I was lost in thought as I pulled into the shared parking lot between Heroes and Villains Comics, We Scream Ice Cream, and Roasted Beans. I could smell the aroma of coffee as I headed into the comic shop.

"Hey, Jess. Welcome," Monte said from behind the counter. He was typing on the computer.

"Hey, Monte. Thanks."

"Here for the new artwork?"

"You know me so well."

"I do." He chuckled as he continued to work on the computer.

I walked to the back wall where the local art was displayed. Starting on the left, I walked slowly looking at each piece. There were a lot of great pieces. Everything from birds and flowers to dragons and elves. An abstract one caught my eye.

It had a mix of swirls and stripes in avocado, harvest gold, and earthy brown of the 1970s. I stopped to examine it closer.

"I thought you might like that one," Monte yelled across the shop. "I almost set it behind the counter for you."

"Yeah, something in it really … speaks to me." I wasn't even born in the 70s, but I was drawn to that decade for some reason. Yes, I also loved dragons and elves, and there were some great ones on the wall today, but I really loved this one.

Checking the corner for the price, it was only eighty. I could swing that. I looked down the entire wall. I hadn't even seen half of the paintings yet. I wanted to look at all of them before I made a decision.

"Want me to hold it," Monte said, coming up next to me.

"Um," I looked around. There wasn't anyone else in the store, but I really wanted it. "Yes, please. I just want to look at the rest really quick, just in case."

"Great. There is an Albert Winston near the end you might like."

I followed his finger. "Thanks. I will look for it."

I looked at the rest of the artwork, but even the Albert Winston didn't speak to me the way that the 1970s abstract by the new-to-me artist did.

Walking up to the counter, I smiled at Monte. He already had it wrapped up in brown paper for me and bagged in one of his oversized logo bags.

"Tell Vee I'm expecting new figures next week."

"I will." I tapped my credit card, thanked him, then took the bag. "Thanks, Monte!"

I walked out. Before I reached my car, I noticed a large group coming out of Roasted Beans. One of the people was familiar. He called out.

"Hey, Jess!" Todd called.

"Hey, Todd. Nice to see you."

He came over, giving me a kiss on the cheek and a quick hug.

"Here, come meet my team. We were just meeting about the Jamison property. Trying to finalize our Plan B and talking about what happened at the city council meeting the other night."

"Oh, okay. Just let me set this in my car." I held up the bag.

"Comic books?" He chuckled.

"Not exactly. They sell local artwork on the back wall. I bought a new piece."

"Oh, nice." He looked over his shoulder at the comic bookstore. "I might have to check that out sometime."

"You should. They have almost everyone." I put the bag carefully in my backseat, then turned to face him and his team who had gathered around my car. They were all staring. I was feeling a bit awkward with them all looking at me. I've competed on TV and in front of live audiences, but this is a whole new level of interaction. "Um, hi."

They laughed.

"Yeah, sorry, that was a little awkward. Hi, I'm Kay Rigby. I'm co-manager on this project with Todd." She reached out to shake my hand.

Kay was the one who gave me a dirty look the other night, but today, she was sweet as syrup. Weird.

The others all introduced themselves. Matt Walker, Jerry Flynn, and Foster Platt were all project members, and Cassidy Flick was the project assistant.

"If they need a copy or a coffee or an opinion, I'm the gal." She laughed. "They would fall apart without me."

"For real."

"Definitely."

"No doubt."

"Well, it's nice to meet you all."

"And Jess is the chef and owner of The Crock Pot restaurant," Todd said.

"Oh, wow! That place has the best biscuits," Kay said.

"I prefer the cornbread," Jerry said.

"The Alphabet soup is my favorite," Matt said.

"I love everything, but the Maxine Iced Tea … de-li-cious!" Cassidy swooned, adding a chef's kiss gesture.

Foster nodded along with everyone, but didn't add his opinion. I got the idea he was a man of few words.

"Wait, you were also on a bunch of those cooking shows, weren't you?" Jerry asked.

"Yeah, you were! I saw you. You were good," Matt added before I could answer.

"Guilty. Yes, that's kind of how I got my start."

They were all amazed and started bombarding me with questions. I tried my best to answer each question, but I might have missed a few. Todd just stood on watching with his classic smirk plastered on his face.

"I can't believe we now know a celebrity," Cassidy finally said. "That's amazing."

"I wouldn't say celebrity. I just got lucky a few times." I smiled.

"Don't they also call you the Crime Fighting Chef?" Foster asked. His voice startled me. He hadn't said a word this entire time.

"Um, yeah, but that's just a silly thing."

"But you do solve crimes, right? Your sous chef, those three people, and then you figured out what was happening at the Caruso's Funeral Home, right? That was all you."

Five heads turned to look from Foster to me.

"I … um, yeah, that was me. It was just dumb luck, though." I said as casually as possible. I looked at each face, trying to read if they believed me.

There was just an awkward silence among the group.

"Well, we better get going, but it was good to run into you," Todd said. "I'll call you later."

Thank you, Todd, I thought.

"Nice to meet you," we all said, except for Todd and Foster.

Foster simply watched me as I climbed into my car and drove away. That stare was an almost menacing expression. What was he thinking? What had I done to him?

My phone rang. It was Vee. They must be off of work.

"Hey, girl. What's up?" I asked.

"We just got off work. What are you thinking about for dinner?" she asked.

"Honestly, I hadn't thought about it yet, but I can stop at the store to grab something."

"I want your chicken cheesy, pepper casserole thingy," Sawyer yelled.

"Oh, yeah, I can do that." It was something I had seen online and then tweaked. I didn't have a name for it, so his description was the most accurate way to ask for it.

"Great. Is there anything you need us to do for you when we get home?"

"Nah, but I just ran into Todd and his project team. That was awkward."

"Really?" Vee asked. "With Todd or his team or both?"

"Mostly just his team member, Foster. He kept staring at me, didn't talk much, and then when he did, he focused on that stupid nickname the media gave me, the Crime Fighting Chef."

"That's weird. Should we add his name to the board?"

I thought for a second.

"Yeah, we probably should, and we can do a little research on him after dinner."

"I'll start once I get changed. Do you know his full name?"

"Yeah, Foster Platt. Thanks."

We hung up. I drove over to the grocery store. It was an uneventful trip, until I was coming out.

"Hey, Jess, right?" someone asked.

"Yes, oh, you're Kay. You work with Todd."

"Yes, that's right. Weird that I would run into you like this."

"Yeah, at a grocery store." I tried to joke, but I guess she took offense as a frown formed.

"I just meant, I only just met you and here I see you again." She crossed her arms.

"Sorry, it was supposed to be a joke. I didn't mean to offend."

She quickly smiled. "Oh, I get it now."

Talk about mood swing, but that has been our very short relationship so far.

"Well, I'll let you get to shopping, but good to see you."

"Yeah, good to see you," she said.

I looked back once as I put the bags in my back seat. She was still standing there. I waved and said a prayer of thanks that thought bubbles didn't appear above my head.

With everything I needed to create the casserole for my roommates, I headed home. When I got there, Sawyer and Vee ran out to help me bring in groceries. It was only a few bags, which I could have easily gotten by myself, but I appreciated the gesture.

"So, quick, before you take a shower, I did a search of that guy Foster Platt."

"Yeah?"

"He has a few posts blasting this renovation. He seems to be friends with some of the folks that are associated with the Dashboard Beautification Organization."

"Really?"

"Yes, so that seems like a conflict of interest, right?"

"Definitely. Did you write it on the board?"

"I did."

"Well, great. We can review it after dinner. I'll go shower and then get started on dinner."

Dinner was awesome. Sawyer cleaned up the kitchen for us while Vee and I moved into the office to review the board.

"Okay, so Foster is friends with Piper Jeans and Nash Willey. They are both in prominent positions." She pointed to the search results on her computer.

"Oh, I see. Um, do you think I should mention it to Todd?"

"Don't you think he knows?"

"Yeah, maybe. I don't really know him all that well yet either, so who knows?" I shrugged.

I thought about my own employees. Would I know if they had affiliation with another chef or restaurant, but did it matter as much in my business?

"I would *definitely* keep an eye on this guy." She tapped his name on the board.

"I think you are right."

We stared at it a few more minutes.

I thought about the weird interaction with Kay. Should I add her to the board or was she just a strange person? If she was just a socially awkward person, that didn't mean she was guilty. I had my moments of foot in mouth disease or times I missed social queues.

Foster had been a little more suspicious in my opinion, then to find out that he had a conflict of interest, it made me think we were right to suspect him.

"It's not much," Vee said.

"No, I need some real clues, not just a list of people and places."

Looking at each other, we shrugged then went into the living room for our usual nightly routine of playing on our phones while Sawyer plays video games.

Chapter Nine

I tossed and turned all night, which was starting to feel almost normal. It was the guilt at not doing more for Marco which was weighing on me. I felt an urgency to solve this.

Tomorrow, Marco had asked for the day off so he could go to group therapy at the VA hospital in Pinehurst, and then he was supposed to meet with his lawyer afterwards.

I also kept thinking about what my aunt and Ms. Edie had shared about how it was affecting his mother, wife, and the rest of his family. I knew I had to do this quickly.

"I'm worried about him," I told Noah earlier. We were watching Marco stomp around the dining room as he cleared tables.

"Yeah, he seems depressed."

"Has he said anything to you?"

"Just to ask for time off. But nothing else," Noah said.

I hated this for Marco. Losing his friend and being the prime suspect, worrying about his mother, problems in his marriage. That is why I was going to look again at the building, especially after Todd's random comment.

So, after work, I headed straight to Jamison, driving slowly as I neared the burned-out building. Not much looked different from the last time I was here.

It still had the caution tape up. I also noticed they had posted some no trespassing signs. They were simple ones on stakes flanking either side of the front door.

There weren't any vehicles in front of the building and no sign that there were workers present, but I decided not to stop in front of it, just in case. Plus, I didn't want to get caught on the cameras in the area. I mean, if I was just driving by, it would be less suspicious, right?

As I looked around, I saw there were a lot of people on the street, not at this building, but going to their homes or to the convenience store on the far corner. Just one more reason not to be seen here.

I continued driving to the end of the block, then turned left to drive around to the next street. I peeked down the alley. No cars were visible behind the building either, and I didn't see anyone in the alley. I continued to Greer Street. It ran parallel to Jamison.

Parking on Greer, this entire street was nearly empty. There were no longer any businesses open here, just for lease signs and long forgotten going out of business announcements. There weren't any people walking around like on Jamison or any of the streets leading here.

I stared out at the building that sat immediately behind the burned building. It used to be Sloane Department store. It was once the favorite place to get back-to-school clothes and had a cafeteria on the third floor where my grandmother would take me to eat.

It was now a sad reminder of what once had been. We still had some stores in town, but more people were starting to opt for online shopping.

As I thought about how eerie this block was, a chill ran through me as the hair on the back of my neck stood up. What was causing my reaction?

I glanced around, half expecting zombies to be creeping towards me, but saw nothing. There were a few birds in the trees that still lined the street. Though, with years of neglect, the trees were overgrown and unkept. Limbs were growing over the street or hitting the eaves of the buildings.

I started looking for any cameras. I saw a few, but with nothing open here, was anyone checking them? Who could access them? Were they even connected to a monitoring system?

I bet if Colt was still alive, he could do it, I thought.

My only option was to ask Detective Upton or maybe Officer Rafferty. They might know.

I climbed out of the car, crossing the vacant street. It was still empty and eerie here. I glanced down the alley that led to the burned building on Jamison. The old Sloane building was on the left and what used to be a tax office on the right. It looked safe enough. There weren't any shadows or places for someone to hide. A few crushed cardboard boxes, a lone bag of trash, but nothing else. Not even a mouse.

"Here goes," I whispered as I stepped into the alley, looking up and down as I walked.

There weren't any cameras that I could see in this area, nor could I see the ones that were pointing on the street. It would have been easy for anyone to slip down this way without being seen, especially if those few cameras that I had seen weren't being monitored.

There were no windows facing this area. It was a weird space, but the perfect place to commit a crime and that's exactly what someone had done.

I reached the back of the burned building. The back door was wide open, damaged during the fire. The frame of the glass door melted and twisted, all the glass blown out.

This is not safe. This is not safe, I thought as I stepped carefully through the glass and over the door frame.

The smell of smoke hit me hard, burning my throat and causing me to gag. It was sharp, acrid, burning the back of my throat. The next smell was almost a damp, musty smell.

I fought every urge in me to run, but because I had to look around for clues, I kept going, breathing carefully as I moved forward.

I could see the scorch marks crawling up the walls. There were definitely spots that looked more damaged, more charred. From my research, that meant arson, though I was no expert. I did a simple Internet search. Plus, I was a fan of true crime shows.

Also, when I had talked to Detective Upton, he had confirmed that there was an accelerant used. He had been impressed that I knew what to look for.

I stepped through the area that had once been a sitting area. It still had furniture in, well, it did before the fire. Now, it was unrecognizable as furniture.

It had once been leather couches and high-back side chairs with cherry wood coffee tables between them.

When Sawyer, Vee, and I used to sneak in here, we would hang out in this area, drinking beers we had swiped from Vee's house. We weren't the only ones who would come here, either. It was a popular hangout. The police kept a close eye on it, so we had all gotten really good at slipping in without ever going in the front.

But that was back in the days when there weren't security cameras on everything. Some stores had them, sure, but not every building and street corner. We could easily make our way through the back alley. That's also why I knew that it was possible to come in that way.

Also, back then, there had been lots of critters running around the building. Rats and mice, roaches and spiders, but now there was nothing. It was creepy and just eerie with how still it was inside.

A chill ran down my spine as I walked around studying this or that, stepping over burned bits of debris and ducking around fallen beams. It was amazing the damage.

"Wow," I mumbled.

As I reached the front of the building, the sky showed through in spots. The fire had moved quickly to the above floors, or maybe it moved down. I actually didn't know how fires worked, especially intentionally set fires like this one.

Though I had learned a bit about arson and what to look for, that was the extent of my knowledge.

I looked up, trying to figure out how the firefighters had gotten to the third floor and found Zach's body, checking, first, the back staircase to find it was blocked by debris. The one in the front was burned up to almost the second floor, so I couldn't go up.

Bummer, I thought as I studied the upper floors. I could see some of it where the fire had caused the floor above to collapse. A morbid thought crossed my mind. What if his body had fallen down here in the fire?

That caused a shiver to once again travel my spine.

I noticed in the far corner there was a large pile of tools, a toolbox, and freshly cut wood. They did not look like they were here during the fire. Probably here from the project team, but from this distance, I couldn't see if there was a name on it.

I started to walk towards them, but before I could examine it more closely, a sudden flutter of wings above me caused bricks to fall. I ducked and covered my head.

Bleep! Maybe I should get out of here.

I took one more look around, eyeing the tools and wood. There was nothing else here that could help me. I have no idea what I thought I would see. I was just so desperate for a clue, or perhaps it was a morbid curiosity to see the destruction that drove me to nose around.

Either way, the flock of birds trying to take me out had me making a run for the exit and there was nothing telling me who had a financial interest in this project.

Back in the alley, I took a deep breath of fresh air. I had gotten used to the rancid smoke smell mixed with the plastic and metals in the building, but I could definitely tell the difference being out here.

As I stood there catching my breath, a loud noise in one of the empty buildings caused the hair on the back of my neck to stand up. That building was empty, or at least appeared empty. Was it a rat, a bird, a person? I didn't know, but I decided I wasn't going to stick around to find out.

With fear as motivation, I practically sprinted back to my car. I hit the unlock button on my fob just before reaching it. I turned to look back, half expecting to see someone or something chasing me. Nothing.

I leaned on my car to take in the full scene again. Was I just being paranoid?

Ugh! I groaned.

Climbing in my car, I gave up. As I drove away, I caught a whiff of myself.

"Ick!" I smelled like the gross fire. Not like a pleasant campfire or romantic fire. No, this was acrid and harsh. I gagged as I hit the window buttons to lower all my windows. "This is never going to come out of my hair or clothes."

Ten minutes later, I pulled up at my townhouse. I couldn't wait to get cleaned up and changed. Not only did I smell like smoke, but I also smelled like the kitchen. Not a great combination. I just hoped it didn't linger in my car.

I didn't see Sawyer's car. Vee's was parked at the curb like usual. Typically, they took his to work.

"Hello?" I yelled when I got inside, just in case. No answer. I called out again. Nothing. *Awesome*.

After verifying that I was alone, I went to the laundry room, stripping out of my smoke-filled clothing and starting them to wash. Then I sprinted upstairs to shower before anyone saw me.

I turned the water on hot, then did the lather, rinse, repeat thing three times before I was satisfied that I'd washed the smoke and food smells off of me. Doing the sniff test, I felt good, so I dried and dressed before heading downstairs.

I sent Vee a text message about dinner, as they should be minutes from heading home. Normally, I didn't mind cooking, but today I wanted a break.

V: **We'll pick something up**

Me: **Thanks!**

Then I got a text from Todd. My stomach flip-flopped as I read it.

T: **Hey, beautiful. Good day?**

Me: **Busy. You?**

T: **Good, good.**

Me: **Glad to hear it**

T: **I'd love to see you again soon**

Me: **I'm free most evenings**

T: **How about tomorrow night then?**

Me: **Sounds good.**

We worked out the details of the date over the next few texts. I was excited. He had suggested Dragon's Alley. I loved that place.

It was just weird enough, and the food was excellent. They also brewed their own beer.

It was decorated exactly how you would imagine. The center piece of the restaurant was a handcrafted dragon that hung in the rafters and its tail wrapped down and around one of the large stone columns in the center. The employees were all dressed in Renaissance era clothing. It was a fun vibe.

While I waited for my friends, I went into the office to stare at the clue board. I added a post-it with the words "TOOLS and WOOD."

My roommates came in the door with the usual gusto and energy.

"Honey, we're home!" They both yelled.

"Hey, y'all!" I shouted from the couch.

"Phew, what is that smell?" Vee gagged.

"You can still smell it?" My clothes were in the wash and should be nearly done. I had even showered, lathering and rinsing three times.

"Yeah, what is that? Is it you?" she said, coming closer to me, sniffing me. "Ew! Did you even shower? Where were you? Smell her."

Sawyer came over, smelling the air around me. His nose wrinkled as he got a whiff of the smoke.

"Holy moly! You reek of smoke." He backed up quickly.

I jumped up, horrified that I still smelled.

"I went to the abandoned building."

"You went inside it?"

"Yeah. It was gross, a disaster on the inside. Just a huge disaster."

"And rancid." Vee screwed her face up. "Did you even shower?"

"Yes! I showered. I soaped up head to toe more than once." The washer buzzed. "And that's my clothes that I was wearing."

I ran to the washer. The smell hit me.

"Holy, bleep! How, how do I get rid of this smell?"

Vee pulled out her phone, typing something in the search.

"Okay, it says add half a cup to a cup of baking soda." She ran to the kitchen, coming back with the box of baking soda and a half a cup. "Here we go."

She dropped in half a cup, then after a sniff, she dropped another half a cup of baking soda in. Then started my clothes again.

"Okay, and then for you … There are a ton of options. You can wash your hair with citrus juice, baking soda, or apple cider vinegar. It also says you can use your hair dryer, but on a cold setting, not heat. The heat will bake it in."

"Okay, I can do that." I grabbed the baking soda, studying it for a second. "Should I try the juice and vinegar too?"

"No, just pick one. You'll make it worse," Vee said. "Oh, and hurry, food is getting cold."

I ran upstairs to take another shower, frustrated at myself for putting myself in that stinky and dangerous place. I cursed myself the entire time, but when I got out, I could tell that I smelled better.

When I joined my friends again, they were setting the table and unloading food.

"Better?" I asked.

They both sniffed me, which is not the weirdest thing we've done together, but it does make the top five list.

"Better," they agreed.

"Now I have to hope my clothes come clean."

We settled down in our seats. They had picked up food from a new Mediterranean Restaurant called Spicy Fig Bistro. They had ordered us a mix of things that included hummus, falafel, salad, and kabobs.

"Alrighty, now tell us why you were at the building and what you found, if anything," Vee said as she scooped a large glob of hummus onto pita bread.

"Nothing much. As I said, it was just a mess. I did notice though that Greer Street in that block is abandoned. All the stores and buildings were empty. No power seemed to be going to them. So, I have to wonder about the cameras in that section of the street."

"Hm, interesting. I wonder if Upton or Rafferty could get information on it," Sawyer said.

"That's what I thought, too. I'll have to text one or both of them."

"Would Todd know?" Vee asked.

"He might, but I honestly don't want him to know I was there."

Even though I'd agreed to a second date with him, I couldn't get Riley's words out of my head. What if he was just using me to learn what I knew or what I found out? I didn't think he was the killer, but there was that nagging thought in my head.

"Makes sense."

"I did find some tools and wood that didn't look like they were there during the fire."

"That could be nothing, though. It's a construction zone," Sawyer said.

"True, and I did think that. Plus, they had some signs out front that looked like they could have been made out of the wood."

"Probably what the wood was for then." Sawyer nodded. His father was a woodworker as a hobby, when he wasn't on the road as a long-haul trucker. In fact, he had built our clue board for us.

"Yeah, but I put it on the board, just in case."

"Good idea," they said in almost unison, then they both yelled "jinx!" which caused a fit of laughter.

"This is really good. Were they busy?" I said. I took a bit of falafel dipped in tzatziki, followed by a hunk of feta.

"Not too busy. I grabbed a menu for you." Vee pointed to the kitchen island.

"Nice. Thanks. I'll check it out."

I liked to support my fellow chefs and restaurant owners. I knew what it took to get me there, and I imagine for many of them it was a similar journey.

After dinner, I sent a text message to Rafferty. For some reason, I didn't want to ask Detective Upton.

Me: **Hey, Raff, what do you know about the security cameras on Greer?**

His reply didn't come right away, but when it did, it was exactly what I thought.

R: **Not working. Why?**

Me: **No reason.**

R: **There is always a reason with you, but don't tell me. I think I can figure out why. Just be careful, please.**
Me: **Will do :)**

He sent me back an eye roll emoji. I didn't reply, but I was glad to have the answer I was expecting. Someone could have snuck in the back of that building. It was the right amount of doubt that could clear Marco. I just had to figure out how to prove it.

Chapter Ten

Todd had to cancel our dinner yesterday, but today we were going to meet after he got off work. It was Wednesday, and I had the day off. My roommates had to work, so I spent the day doing chores and organizing my room a bit.

Then I made a pot of chicken and dumplings, so my friends had dinner. That way, they could come home to something nice. The soup could sit most of the afternoon and I would just drop the dumplings in right before serving.

"Hey, we're home," Vee called.

I have to admit, I was mildly disappointed when they didn't burst in with the same line each day, but fine.

"Hey, y'all!"

"Oh, wow, it smells so good. Did you cook us dinner?" Sawyer asked, coming to peek.

"Yes, I had time and thought y'all would enjoy it."

"Definitely smells better than that smoke from the other day." Vee faked a gag sound.

"Ha, ha. I just have to drop the dumplings and then I'm heading out."

"You look nice," Vee said, hugging me.

"Thanks." I looked down at my outfit. It was Army green baggy slacks with a vintage band shirt, chunky sandals, and a long silver necklace with a large evil eye pendent. It was casual, but very much my style. "So, you think it is okay for a date?"

"I already told you, don't try to be someone you aren't, Jess. You have done that for a guy before."

"Aaron," Sawyer and I said in unison.

"Yes, Aaron. You were miserable trying to be what he wanted. Crisp blouses, slacks, and pumps. No art, no music. You weren't happy."

"Yeah, I'm glad that didn't last long," I mumbled. "But you are right. Screw it. This is me."

"Good for you."

"I'm going to go change before dinner." Sawyer kissed my forehead, then darted upstairs.

"Why don't you go change, too? I'll just get the dumplings in while y'all do that," I said to Vee.

She grinned and followed Sawyer up the stairs.

I turned up the heat on the pot so it could boil. Next, I mixed up the batter for the dumplings. Once the soup was rolling, I scooped out golf ball sized dough, dropping them quickly into the broth. Ten minutes later, they were perfect.

"Okay, friends, I'm out of here. Soup is ready. I hope you enjoy it."

"Oh, we will," Sawyer said as he grabbed a ladle full.

"Have fun!" Vee yelled.

"I will."

I hopped in my car and turned on the radio. One of my favorite songs happened to be on. I cranked it up.

"Perfect."

To get to Dragon's Alley, I would need to drive by city hall.

Wouldn't it be funny if I saw Todd as he was leaving? I thought.

As I got closer, I saw a crowd ahead of me. They were blocking the road. There were police standing nearby, and the crowd held signs and posters as they chanted. That's when it dawned on me. It was a protest.

I could read some of the signs, but I couldn't quite tell what they were chanting. It might have been a mix of what was on the signs, but they weren't on the same page.

Park. Not concrete!

Tear it to the ground!

Todd Barber must go

Fire Todd!

Dashwood Beautification NOW

Mayor Lackland is tone deaf

After doing research into this group the other night, I knew they believed that a park would be better for the environment and for keeping the small town feel. They hated Todd and his development company for taking his on and at the mayor for approving the zoning. It wasn't just her decision, but from what I could tell, this group was radical and wanted a scapegoat or two.

The police had a barricade in place, so I was going to have to turn and go a different route. Curiosity took over when I saw Rafferty, not far away.

I pulled my car into a nearby parking spot and then walked over to where my friend stood.

"Hey, Raff."

"Oh, hey, Jess. Look at you. What are you dressed for?"

"Date."

"Didn't realize you did that."

"Yeah, ha." I couldn't tell if he was joking, but I laughed, just in case. "So, what's this about?"

"Ah, yeah, protesting the Jamison Heights Complex. They have been at it for about an hour now."

"Oh, wow." I turned to watch as the crowd started booing.

Todd was coming out of the door with Chief Stone and Officer Perez providing security. They escorted him safely to his car as the crowd pushed to reach him.

"They *do not like* that guy," Raff laughed.

"That's the guy I'm meeting for dinner," I mumbled.

"Really? Ha. Good luck."

"Gee, thanks." I watched as Todd got to his car.

Chief and Perez stood there while he drove off. The protesters ran to his car, shaking it and shouting. Raff and other officers from all around ran to push back the crowd and secure the scene while Todd escaped. I watched in an almost awe-like horror. That was only something I had seen on television.

I watched as the crowd got wilder now that the police had let Todd go. That was my sign to leave. I needed to get going, anyway.

Before I arrived, I got a text. Thankfully, my car could read it for me. It was Todd letting me know he had arrived. A slow smile crept across my face and a warmth formed on my cheeks.

"Reply. Almost there." The car confirmed, and I told it to send. I giggled slightly, then chastised myself a bit at the ridiculous crush. I hadn't known him for very long, but I still got giddy when we talked or saw each other.

Silly girl. I laughed at myself.

A few minutes later, I pulled into Dragon's Alley. The parking lot was about half full. I saw Todd's car. I hopped out, looked down at my outfit again. Why was I so nervous? I almost never worried about my clothes either.

Oh well. Here goes.

I stepped inside to the smoky smell of an open fire, savory meat aroma, and festive ambiance of a Ren Faire.

"Huzzah!" the host at the door shouted.

"Huzzah," I said back.

"Hey, Chef. You're here to meet someone, right?" he asked.

"I am."

"Follow me." He nodded, grabbing a menu and napkin bundle.

Todd stood when we got to the table.

"Hey." I smiled.

"Hey, yourself."

We took our seats, and the host left us with the menus and a promise that our server would be right over. In less than a second, and before Todd and I could speak, the server came to take our drink orders and read us the specials. Once she left, we were finally able to talk.

"Hi. You look nice." He smiled.

"Thanks. So do you."

He was dressed in business casual, with a short-sleeved button-down blue plaid shirt with khakis. It didn't quite fit the themed restaurant, but neither did mine.

"I'm glad you were able to meet. I almost thought I would have to cancel," He said.

"The protesters?"

"Yeah. How did you know?"

"I was there."

"Oh, are you one of the protesters?" His eyes narrowed as he looked me up and down.

"No, not me, but it is on my route to the restaurant. I had to take the long way."

His eyes softened at my reply. He nodded.

"Ah, yeah, so you saw. It was a madhouse. They had to escort me out of there and even then, the protesters nearly got me."

"That sounds scary." I stopped myself from sharing that I was there watching him. Not sure why, but it felt creepy. It wasn't like I was there spying, but it might come across that way.

"That Kimberly Gibbs has it out for me and this project."

"Who is she?"

"She's the leader of Dashwood Beautification Organization. They are the ones trying to get the park in place of the building."

"Ah, okay. I didn't remember her name." I had only done limited research on that group after finding that Foster Platt had an association with the group.

Our drinks arrived, and we ordered our dinners. With that bit of business out of the way, we got back to our conversation.

"I swear she is the one who set the fire. I just can't prove it." He looked at me. "Have you heard anything new?"

"No, nothing. Why do you think it is her?"

"Well, I would start with Kimberly and her crew, Piper and Nash. Those two would do anything, and I mean, anything, to please her." He took a long sip of his beer.

"Have you mentioned it to the police?"

"Yeah, but they are sticking with your guy." He exhaled heavily. "It's stupid. It can't be him."

"Why do you say that?"

"Too obvious. Right? I mean, your guy was caught on camera going in. That just seems too … I don't know, easy. A murder and arson would be done more under the radar. Don't you think?"

I thought about the past investigations. Yeah, I guess some criminals knew how to hide. It made sense to me, but I also knew that many criminals were caught on camera. So, I guess I just talked myself out of believing his theory, even if it told the story I wanted it to.

Ugh!

"So, what do you think?" he asked.

"Honestly, I don't know. I do believe that Marco didn't do it, but I just have no proof and no other leads."

"I gave you at least three. Look into them and it could get your guy off the suspect list."

I cringed each time he referred to Marco as my guy. He was my employee and friend, but that was all.

"Well, I'll have to look into them because I want to help my employee."

"Good." He sat back. "So, how is work going? Business is good?"

"Um, yeah, so good."

"Anything new on the menu?"

"Not really. I guess with it being fall now, we have been selling a lot of our chicken and dumplings."

"Oh, I had that the other day. It was so good."

"I'm glad you enjoyed it."

The rest of the evening went on with no more talk about the murder or the beautification organization, but my mind kept taking me back to that topic. I wanted to pick up my phone to search for each person on the organization and their cause. Get some information and look for a motive. I couldn't understand why they thought burning the building would help get a park, but maybe they believed it would buy them more time to argue their case.

Maybe they had something else in the works. I had no idea, but I couldn't wait to look into it.

I realized my mind had wandered a bit, and I wasn't listening to Todd. As quickly as I had that thought, I saw he was staring at me with an odd smirk.

"What's that for?" I laughed nervously, brushing a strand of hair behind my ear.

"You were deep in thought, so I was just watching. Your face is expressive." He chuckled softly.

My face burned with embarrassment. I had been told that I wear my thoughts. It was something I needed to work on.

"Yeah, sorry. Just thinking about work." I don't know why I lied. I guess I still didn't trust him fully. Plus, it didn't help that Riley's words still lived rent free in my head.

"What if he is the killer? He could be trying to get close to you."

Trying to ignore my self-doubts and insecurities, I smiled as I studied him, trying to gage my lie. Had he bought it?

"I bet. It probably takes a lot to run your own restaurant."

"Yes, so much to think about. At least I have a great staff and my managers are amazing."

Soon after, we ended our date. He paid the bill, and we walked out to our cars together. As we were stepping out of the restaurant, a familiar face came into sight.

"Hey, Todd!" Foster said, then his face fell into a scowl when he saw me.

"Hey, my man Foster. How's it going?"

"Good. Good." He eyed me. "What are you doing here?"

"We just had a nice date." Todd smiled at me, taking my hand.

"With her? You know she is trying to prove you murdered that homeless veteran, right?"

Todd dropped my hand and looked at me as if I slapped him.

"Why would you say that?" I asked Foster. "I never…"

"Why else would you be dating him? You have nothing in common."

"Is that true? You are investigating me?" Todd asked me, completely ignoring Foster.

"No, no. I'm just trying to prove my employee didn't do it, unless you did, which I don't believe."

He took my hand again, giving it a light squeeze, then turned to his team member.

"Foster, I'm not sure why you think that, but I hope that you will apologize to Jessica."

"Look, I'm not exactly sorry. I don't trust her, but I'm sorry that I said it out loud."

Todd squeezed my hand harder.

"We'll discuss it at work."

He pulled me to the parking lot. I looked over my shoulder just as Foster lifted his middle finger.

Classy. Not.

"I'm glad that you could meet for dinner. It was fun." He stepped forward, taking my hand. "I'm so sorry for Foster. I think the stress is causing him to lash out a bit."

"I understand. Stress can make us all a bit crazy."

Though, honestly, I wanted to be less gracious about Foster's rudeness. I really wanted to tear him a new one, but that just wasn't my personality.

"I'd love to see you again soon."

"I'd like that." I smiled.

He gave me a soft kiss before opening my car door for me. Stunned slightly by his actions, because I wasn't used to this kind of treatment from a date, he whispered goodbye, then shut my door.

I drove away thinking about how much of a gentleman he seemed to be. To date, I have only dated jerks. Except maybe Colt, but unfortunately, I never got to know him past a few phone calls and a week's worth of text messages, since he was killed on the way to our first date. My imagination had painted him positively, though, especially as I dug into his life while investigating his murder.

I barely remember the ride home as I replayed the entire date. Had I been awkward? Would there be a third date? Was he the killer? All the normal after date thoughts.

I couldn't shake the weirdness with Foster either, but I tried to push that negative out of my mind for the moment. I wanted to savor the positive aspects of the date.

Did I still consider Todd a suspect? I couldn't believe that the person I went on a date with could be the same person who killed Zach Boyd and set fire to the Jamison Avenue building. This man was the nicest person, considerate, and fun to be with. We had good conversations on music and art. He liked trying new foods. He actually listened when I talked.

By the time I parked at my house, I had convinced myself that I was being crazy to even suspect Todd. So that meant it had to be someone from the Dashwood Beautification Organization, right? I sprinted inside so I could start my research on them.

"How was the date?" Vee asked, running to meet me.

"Um, it was good."

"Just good?" She laughed.

"Ha, yeah," I chuckled. "Actually, it was pretty good."

"Third date?"

"We didn't make any official plans, but yes, tentatively. I also have some potential leads for Zach's murder."

"Really? How did that come up?"

I explained about the protesters and then how Todd suggested them. I didn't mention Foster yet. I would, but I wanted to sit on it for a minute. I'm not sure why.

"His exact words were focused on Piper and Nash, that they would do anything to please Kimberly, who is the head of the organization."

"Oh, anything could mean murder."

"Yeah. Wanna help me research?"

"You know I do! Want some herbal to go with the verbal?"

"What?"

"Tea? You know, tea means the drink and gossip. Herbal is drink, verbal is the gossip."

"Oh," I smiled.

"I guess since I had to explain it, it isn't funny any longer." She pouted. "I thought it was funny."

"It was! I'm sorry I missed the punchline."

"Was that a yes to the tea, the drink kind?"

"Yes."

I grabbed my laptop, and we sat at our kitchen island. I tapped in the organization's name into the search box. There were several hits, but the first one was the website for the Dashwood Beautification Organization. I clicked the link.

The first image to show was Jamison Heights Complex with a big red X across it. It was a strange centerpiece.

"That's a weird picture," Sawyer said, coming up behind me. He leaned down to see better. "This is their website?"

"Yeah."

Vee came over carrying our mugs of tea.

"Oh, that's kinda grotesque, right?" she asked, taking the seat next to me.

"It is. Okay, so here is Kimberly. She's the chairperson of the organization. Todd thinks she is a prime suspect."

I studied her face for a moment. I had always been good with faces, but I don't remember seeing her at the city council meeting or in the crowd earlier in front of city hall. Granted it was a large crowd, so who knows? Maybe she was there.

I clicked on her biography.

It was just standard stuff. Nothing that screamed killer or at least led me to think she could have done it.

She graduated college with a bachelor's in project management and a master's in architecture. She has worked in New York, Washington, D. C., and Baltimore in multiple city positions and projects. Her resume included many city renovation projects.

Piper was her administrative assistant and had been with Kimberly since Baltimore, from what I could tell. Prior to that, it lists that she worked on several political committees in D.C.. She also had assisted a few senators on major beautification and restoration projects.

Nash was the co-chairperson. He was a civil engineer. Most of his projects took place in California, restoring areas burned by wildfires or destroyed by mudslides.

"They have impressive resumes," Vee commented.

"Yeah, they do, but obviously they wouldn't have their crime resumes here."

"Touche," she chuckled. "So social media?"

"To the socials."

I tapped and clicked as we looked through all the various places, Facebook to X to Instagram, and everything in between. There were pictures from today's protest and lots of angry followers commenting hate-filled messages aimed towards city hall and Todd.

"Wow, they really don't like Todd," I mumbled.

"No, they do not. But it doesn't make sense."

"No, not at all. It isn't like some of these other places with money hungry people trying to push people out. That building, heck almost the entire area over there, is abandoned. It could use revitalization. It might bring life back into the area," I said.

"True, true. I always liked that old building, though," Sawyer said.

"You just remember drinking and goofing off in it," I teased.

"Yeah, good times."

"It was good times." Vee laughed.

"I just don't really see anything that says murderer here but definitely need to keep an eye on these folks."

My phone rang. The display read Shayla.

She was one of my apprentices that I employed from the culinary arts high school. That is where I had gotten my start and my old teacher and mentor, Mr. Duncan Jones, was still the instructor at the school.

"Hello?"

"Chef?" a tearful voice asked.

"Shayla, are you okay?"

"Yes, nooo." She burst into tears. "I hate to ask, but can you come get me?"

"Of course. Where are you?"

She gave me the name of a convenience store not far from her house. I told her I would be there in a minute.

"Need us to come?" Sawyer asked.

"No, I better go alone. She doesn't really know y'all."

"Let me know what you need. We're here," Vee added as I ran out the door.

Minutes later, I pulled up at the store, but didn't see Shayla. I parked on the end and started to get out, when a shadow came from the side of the building. Hunched shoulders, dragging feet. It was Shayla.

It wasn't until she came into the light that I knew my whole night was about to change direction.

Chapter Eleven

I yawned as I woke up in the uncomfortable chair I had spent the night in. Hospitals should have more comfortable chairs in their rooms.

I tried to be careful as I sat up, stretching. I didn't want to wake Shayla, but I needed to adjust my stiff body. Poor thing was finally asleep after all the tears, exams, and questions.

Her stepfather had really done a number on her. She had a broken rib, two black eyes, and multiple other bruises and cuts.

We were waiting now to hear from the doctors if she could be discharged. I assumed they wouldn't have a problem with it. There was no real reason to keep her longer. The biggest question would be where she would live.

I had offered my place. We would see if the police and her mother were okay with that. Though, based on her mother's behavior last night, I didn't think it was going to be a problem.

When we first got here last night, they called the police to report the abuse. Officer Perez came to take her statement and pictures of the injuries.

I'm glad they sent Officer Lupe Perez. She was a firm, but calm, gentle person. She gave the right amount of care and understanding for this delicate situation, but with the authority to garner respect and get results.

While she gathered the evidence, they sent other officers to pick up her stepfather. My understanding is that he was currently sitting in jail. However, her mother came up to the hospital not to comfort but to yell at Shayla.

She waited until the officers had stepped out, but unfortunately, I was still in the room. I tried with all my might to blend into the wall while they argued, but I heard all of it.

"This is all your fault! If you wouldn't argue and be disrespectful to him, this wouldn't happen!"

"Momma, it isn't my fault. I didn't start it. I'm just a child," Shayla cried.

"You are just … just too willful and disrespectful. Always talking back!"

"And that's a reason for him to beat me? Look at me. Look at me, momma!"

Her mother sighed heavily, stomped her foot, before slowly looking at her. I guess she couldn't come up with a rebuttal, but the proof of her failed parenting was all over Shayla's face.

"I'm going to bail him out later today and when I do, you *shouldn't* be home!"

With that, her mother left. Shayla fought back tears as she looked at me.

"You can stay with me for as long as you need." I smiled.

"I can't ask that of you."

"You aren't asking. I'm offering this to you. You can come stay with me." I stepped over, taking her hand.

"Thank you, Chef."

"We aren't in the kitchen. Call me Jess."

"Thank you, Jess." She smiled for the first time in almost twelve hours.

While Shayla was resting, I left the room to stretch my legs and take care of some business.

I started by sending a message to Vee, asking her for help to get the office ready for Shayla. She replied she would. It had our big murder board in it, but I could explain that. Shayla would understand.

Plus, it had a pullout couch and was semi-private. That was easy to fix as well.

V: **I'll add a curtain to the door**

Me: **Perfect!**

I also coordinated with Parker and Noah to cover my shift at the restaurant, and to find someone for Shayla through Monday, at least. I then called Mr. Duncan Jones, my mentor and the culinary arts teacher at the high school where Shayla still attended. I wanted to report her absence for a few days.

"I am so sorry to hear. Poor Shayla. Let me know if you need anything while she's with you," Mr. Jones said.

"I will. Thanks, Mr. Jones."

With all of that done, I headed to the coffee shop for a coffee, a juice for Shayla, and a couple of pastries.

"Oh Jess, you didn't have to do that. They brought me breakfast."

"I know, but just a little treat." I set the juice and pastry on the table next to her. "These aren't as good as what you and Nat make, but for a hospital, this one has some pretty decent pastries."

She took a bite. "This is pretty good, but yeah, not as good as mine. I'm kind of a superstar."

"Yes, you are." I laughed with her. I was glad to see she was getting herself back.

We sat watching the game show channel until about mid-morning when the doctor came around to check on her. We got the green light to be discharged. Shayla smiled at the news, but I could see a cloud cross through her eyes. I knew she must be thinking of the long road she had ahead.

There was nothing I could say to make it better. All I could do was be there for her and give her a safe place.

Officer Perez stopped by as we were waiting for the discharge papers.

"Report has been filed. We have a restraining order. I will escort you home so you can grab clothing, which your mother has agreed to allow."

"Okay. She had said something about him getting bailed out?"

"Won't happen today, but again, I will be with you, so even if he was there, I could deescalate the situation or get you out of there."

Shayla looked at me.

"I'll be there with you, too."

"Okay," she mumbled. "I really don't want to see my mom."

"I can have another officer meet us there. They can keep her out of the way while you gather what you need."

She took a deep breath, looking from Officer Perez to me.

"No, it's okay. I can do it."

The only problem was there were two cars. So, after some discussion, it was decided that Shayla would go with Officer Perez, and I would meet them there in my car.

We had to wait another hour before the discharge paperwork came. The nurse gave her a prescription for pain medicine and after-care instructions.

"I don't have money to pay for this," she whispered to me.

"Not to worry. All of this is covered," I said.

"You're really too generous. You barely know me."

"I was you once upon a time, in some ways, so yeah, I know you."

Tears filled her eyes, but she looked away before they fell. I could understand her feelings. In our business, tears were often a sign of weakness. I had worked in kitchens where the executive chef would eat you alive for crying.

We parted ways at the parking lot.

"I'll grab your med and meet you at your house. Okay?"

"Okay."

When I got to my car, I hit the button for Vee.

"Hey, Jess! Are y'all on your way?"

"Sort of. We were just discharged, and Lupe Perez took her home to grab clothes and stuff. Is your brother still at work?"

"He should be. Does she need meds?"

"Yeah, and I'm not sure they will allow me to pick them up for a minor who I'm not related to, so I thought I'd call in a favor, maybe." I chuckled.

"Ha, yeah, I get it. Let me call him and I'll call you right back."

It was good to know people in helpful and powerful places. Declan had known me most of my life, so he would know that I had no intention of taking her medicine. If I was picking it up for Shayla, that is exactly who it would go to.

As I pulled out of the parking lot, Vee called back.

"He is there and expecting you."

"Great! Thank you so much. How are things at the house?"

"Everything is ready for our guest. I think she is going to like it."

"I bet she will. Well, I'll see you soon."

"Oh, Sawyer is going to pick up dinner."

"Perfect. Thank you both for being such awesome friends."

"We got you."

I got to Dashwood Community Pharmacy a short time later. I jogged in, nearly running into someone.

"Oh, excuse me." I then recognized her as Piper from the Dashwood Beautification Organization.

"No, excuse me. I was rushing around … oh, hey aren't you Chef Jessica from The Crock Pot?"

"I am." Should I say I know her, too? No, that seemed creepy. Lots of people knew me from the cooking competitions and/or from my restaurant.

"You're dating Todd Barber, right?" Her tone changed to almost a growl as she said his name.

"I wouldn't say dating. Just two dates."

She looked me up and down with an odd smirk on her face.

"He really doesn't have a type, does he?" she snickered.

"What's that supposed to mean?"

"I'm sure you can figure it out."

"So, why do you have such a problem with Todd?"

She stepped closer, lowering her voice. "Just don't trust him. He's a snake and will stop at nothing for his cause."

With that, she flipped her hair and stomped out the door. I had no time to think of a comeback or even to question her further before she was gone.

Bleep. I always thought of the perfect thing to say after the person was gone. I hadn't yet thought of anything, but I'm sure at 2 am I would. I shrugged and went to the back counter to find Declan.

"Hey, hey, Jessie!"

I turned to face the familiar voice. Declan Paz was nearly the complete opposite of his younger sister. Where Vee was short and stout, Declan was tall and lean. Vee had their mother's fair complexion, while Dex had their father's darker one. But they both had the crazy, hard to control hair. Dex just wore it better. Perhaps because he kept it shorter than Vee, or maybe he just knew how to style it.

He came around the counter, grabbing me into a bear hug.

"Hey, Dex. How's it going?" I asked when the hug ended.

"I can't complain. How are you? It's been a minute since I've seen you."

"I'm good. Well, life, you know." I handed him the prescription.

"Ah, yes. Vee told me about the girl. That is heartbreaking." He took it. "I got you."

"You're a saint, no matter what your sister says."

"She's a liar." He chuckled as he stepped back behind the counter to get to work. I leaned against the counter, watching as he worked. After only a few minutes, he handed me a bag. "There you are. These will cause drowsiness so no driving, no using heavy machines. You know the standards. Give me a call if you have any questions about it."

"Thank you so much for this. I really appreciate it."

"Of course. Happy to help a friend."

I took the bag and left. Stepping out into the parking lot, I saw Foster. Our eyes locked. A curse crossed his lips as he jumped into a waiting car, flashing me his middle finger before the door closed. The glare from the sun was in just the right spot that I couldn't tell who the driver was. They left quickly.

I ran to my car hoping to follow, but they were long gone by the time my car was in drive.

"Darn it. Oh well, I need to get to Shayla's anyway," I said.

When I arrived, her mother was sitting outside, smoking. The police car was still out front, so I knew Officer Perez and Shayla were still here.

"May I go in?" I asked her.

"Might as well. I'm not welcome in there." She snuffed out her cigarette, immediately lighting another.

I really wanted to lecture her about standing up for her daughter, not siding with a man or even herself. Why did some parents have to be so selfish? I wasn't a parent myself, so some would say I didn't understand, but honestly, that was one reason I didn't want to be a parent.

When I stepped into the house, it smelled like stale beer, mold, and smoke. I heard voices in a back room.

"Hello? Shayla?" I called out.

"Back here, Chef … err … I mean Jess."

Walking through the house, I was shocked by the state of it, though I really shouldn't have been. There was almost no furniture, only a sunken couch with mismatched cushions. Next to it was a well-worn recliner with a thin throw blanket covering it. There was a coffee table with water stains piled with beer cans and bottles. Along one wall, there were piles of trash. Next to that was a low table with a top-of-the-line brand-new 70-inch television.

Someone's priorities were out of whack here, but who am I to judge?

There weren't any personal touches to make it feel like a home, like kids' artwork or family pictures. Even though she had younger siblings, there was no sign of toys or clothing to suggest they lived here.

Had my grandmother and aunt not stepped in, this could have been my life. At least until my mother met Samuel and got her life on track. Before she married Sam, she lived on her couch in a deep depression, not caring about her hygiene or mine.

I made my way to a nearly bare bedroom. There was a threadbare mattress on the floor with a thin sheet on it. Clothes were piled in milk crates and cardboard boxes. The walls were yellowed and stained.

I knew she didn't have a stable home, but I hadn't realized just how bad it was here. I thought of our office at home. It was going to be much cozier for her than this. Vee would ensure that.

Officer Perez stood nearby as if she was ready to spring into action. She nodded to me when I came into the room.

"Hi. I got your meds. How's it going here?"

"Almost done. I just need to make sure I have all my school stuff," Shayla said, a forced smile on her face.

She had a small pile of clothing on the bed and a couple of grocery bags filled up with clothing. Next to that, she had a backpack. It was well loved and way past its prime. That must be for school. She was digging through a laundry basket. I saw a pair of chef pants which she grabbed and shoved into one of the bags.

"Great. Can I help? Do you want me to take your bags to my car?" I picked up two of them.

"That would be great. Thank you."

I headed to my car. Her mother mumbled as I walked by, but I didn't understand what she said. I ignored her as I popped the trunk and put the bags inside.

"She's gonna give you problems, too, ya know?" Her mom grumbled as I was walking back in. This time I heard her clearly and I just couldn't hold my tongue any longer.

"I think it will be okay."

"Well, y'all need to hurry up. I need to go visit my husband, since they aren't letting him out today."

I should have kept walking. I really should have. Over the years, I had learned that popping off never got me anywhere. But I just couldn't hold this in any longer.

"You know he beat the crap out of your child. *Your child!* You should be on her side. Not his! You are *the* parent and should love her unconditionally, be her protector, and want the best for her. Not this! Not to have her beat up and sent to the hospital."

Her mouth fell open, causing her cigarette to fall to the ground. She made a strangled sound, but didn't say a word.

I turned to go back inside, but saw that Shayla and Officer Perez were standing at the door. I hope they hadn't heard what I said, but by the look on their faces, I think they did.

Clearing my throat, I asked, "ready?"

"Yes." Shayla's voice caught.

"Are you coming with us?" I asked Officer Perez.

She looked over her shoulder at Shayla's mother, but then back to me. "Yeah, I'll just follow to make sure you get there without incident. Though I expect it will be fine."

"Okay, well, let's go."

We put her last two grocery bags into the trunk with the other two, then climbed into the front. She put her backpack on the floorboard in front of her.

We drove away quietly for a moment or two. I needed to tell her about the room before we got there, but I didn't know how to bring it up.

"Thank you for doing this," she said, breaking the silence.

"Of course." I smiled. This gave me an opportunity to bring up the room. "But I do need to tell you something weird about the room we will have you in."

"You saw my bedroom, right? Can't be worse."

"No, it is going to be great, but … you know how they call me the Crime Fighting Chef?"

"Yeah?"

"Well, that room is … that room is the one where we have our clue board."

"Really?" She swung around to face me, becoming animated, even though she winced at her painful ribs. "That is so cool! Maybe I can help you solve it?"

"Maybe."

"I'm so worried about Marco. He is not himself at all. He used to tell me the worst or really best dad jokes. Now he doesn't even smile anymore."

"I noticed."

"Everyone is talking about it."

"Everyone?"

"Yes, they are all worried about him. You know his wife left him?"

"I did not." Though I shouldn't be surprised based on what my Auntie Rita said about his mother and wife being so upset. I'd need to touch base with her to see what she knew.

"Yeah, he's even more upset than before."

"I'll talk to him."

I had no idea what I would say or how I could help, but he was one of my employees. I felt a responsibility to them. Just like Earl, just like Shayla. I wanted to help them. I'd come up with something when the time was right.

We pulled up at my house a moment later. Officer Perez pulled in behind me. Sawyer and Vee came to the door to greet us.

"Okay, looks like everything is good. You have my number if you need me," Officer Perez said.

"Yes, we do. Thank you, Lupe." I smiled.

She smiled, shaking my hand, before driving away. I watched her go.

We grabbed Shayla's bags from the car, then made our way up to the front door.

"Welcome, Shayla. I'm Vee. This is Sawyer."

"Hi," Shayla mumbled, not quite looking up. It had taken her time to warm up to me, but I hoped she would open up to them quicker than that.

"Let me show you to your room," I said.

Sawyer grabbed her bags from her. "Here, let me take that for you."

"No, I ... "

"It's okay. We're here for you," he said with a wink.

"Okay, thank you." She followed us.

We stepped into the office. I was blown away by what Vee had done. Not only had she added a floral curtain to the French door leading into it, which would add some privacy, but she added floral prints to the walls.

She pulled in an extra dresser. On top of it, she added a stand mirror and a few candles. Then, over the window, she added fairy lights to the curtain.

Next to the couch, she added an end table with a lamp.

Lulu jumped on to the bed and meowed up at Shayla. She was a good cat. Shayla leaned over, picking her up.

With tears in her eyes, she whispered, "I get to stay here."

"Yes, this is all for you."

"This is ... too much."

"Not at all. This is your new safe space," I said, putting my arm gently around her.

"I will be so quiet y'all won't even know I'm here."

"Well, right now, we have dinner, so don't be too quiet." Sawyer chuckled.

With that, we started our first night with a teenager.

Chapter Twelve

The doctor ordered Shayla to rest for a few days. I didn't want her home alone. I toyed with the idea of taking the day off, but thankfully it was a government holiday, so Vee and Sawyer would be home with her.

"How did you sleep?" I asked as I made breakfast.

"So good. Best sleep in a long time."

"I'm glad to hear it."

I set a plate piled with migas in front of her, then set the salsa close by.

"Thanks, Jess." She took a bite. "Ohmygosh. This is so good."

"I'm glad you like it."

"I smell food," Vee said, coming downstairs. "Migas!"

"Help yourself," I said. "What are y'all going to do today?"

"I think we'll just hang out and watch movies. What do you think, Shayla? Does that sound good to you?"

"I have a little homework to do, but then yes, movie day sounds perf."

"You have all weekend for homework," Vee said as she took a seat next to our guest.

"I could be convinced to skip it for the day." Shayla laughed.

Last night over dinner, my roommates had made Shayla comfortable and brought her out of her shell. By bedtime, it was like she had lived here for years.

I finished my breakfast, rinsing my plate. "Well, I better get going. I want to get in a little early today."

"Have fun!"

"Tell everyone I will miss them, and I'll see them Monday."

I headed over to the restaurant. My mind was focused on the case. I was trying to sort through the clues. We had Todd pointing his finger at the Dashwood Beautification Organization and they were pointing fingers back at him. It was like little children in a fight.

I still hadn't figured out a motive for either side to go this crazy over a building or a park. At least not enough to try to burn the building down and kill a man. Why would Todd burn the building down? And what did Zach Boyd have to do with any of it? Had he been an unfortunate casualty?

Then you had Foster, who just seemed angry at me, even though we had just met. He had a conflict of interest in working at Todd's development company and being associated with the beautification organization. Though I hadn't seen him marching with the protester and he had been seated with Todd at the city council meeting.

It was just a mixed-up mess without anything solid. I hit the steering wheel. I just wanted some solid clues, not trying to piece this together from nothing. What did I have, a few names and a burned building? Oh, and those tools and wood that had been in the corner. But as Sawyer pointed out, it was a construction site.

"Bleep!" *Too many questions, not enough answers.*

Maybe I should go back to the building? I hadn't tried very hard to go upstairs. The stairs looked like a mangled mess, but there had to be a way. Zach's body was found on the third floor. After I was there the other day, I confirmed he hadn't fallen to the ground floor.

The smart part of my brain said the firefighters had ladders. I didn't, unless you count the two-step stool we had at work. I didn't count it though.

As I rounded the corner to face The Crock Pot, I noticed a small crowd had formed at the front of our building. They had signs and were chanting something that I couldn't quite make out.

What in the world now? Were they protesting my restaurant?

I pulled into our parking lot, then walked around to the front, cell phone in hand in case things got out of control. When they saw me, they started yelling and advancing on me. Instinctively, I took a few steps back.

"No to Todd Barber! No to a building."

"We want a park, not another building!"

Well, alrighty, I had nothing to do with that.

I scanned the faces trying to find any of the leadership for the organization. I didn't see Kimberly, but Piper stepped through the crowd with a huge smirk on her face.

"Hey, Todd Barber's girlfriend. How do you like our cause now?"

"I have never argued against your cause," I countered. "Why are you here? I have nothing to do with the project."

"We need to be heard, and we hear your restaurant is the place to be." She looked over her shoulder for validation. The crowd cheered. "Plus, you *are* dating Todd, right? That's what you told me yesterday."

"You can't protest here."

"This is public space. We can."

"We open at 11. I want y'all gone by then." It was only eight, so hopefully they would tire out by then. I turned to go back inside, but Piper was not ready to be done with me.

"Don't you go. We need you to listen. Get them to stop the project!"

"Why do you think I have any power? I'm just a chef."

"Talk to Todd. I'm sure he will listen to you."

"Like I told you yesterday, it was two dates. I barely know him."

"Well, right now, you have his attention. Just use it to our advantage." She smirked.

I sighed. I could tell I would not win.

"If I promise to at least talk to him, will you leave?"

She looked over her shoulder. "Sure. Talk to him and we'll leave."

I had a feeling I was being played a bit, but I had no choice. If calling him meant a stop to this madness, I was all for it. Plus, I came in early for a reason. Each minute dealing with this was stalling my work.

"Fine." I pulled out my phone, hit the number for Todd. I flashed her the phone so she could see I had dialed his number. "Voicemail … Hey, Todd. It's Jess. I wanted to talk to you about the Jamison Heights Complex project. Give me a call back when you have time. Thanks." I hit the disconnect button, then looked at her. "Happy?"

"Fine," she growled. "Not perfect, but we'll take it. For now. Let's pack it up."

I watched as they slowly dispersed. When I say slowly, it was like watching a snail convention. Piper and some guy were the last to leave.

"By the way, this is Nash. He is the co-chair of our organization."

He didn't look like the picture on the website at all. Piper's picture at least looked like her. Nash was easily ten years older than his picture and fifty pounds heavier with less hair. But in the right light, I supposed, the smile looked the same.

"Nice to meet you," I said, flashing a fake smile. *You catch more flies with honey, right?*

"Nice to meet you as well. We hope to hear good news from *your* conversation." His words were sharp, almost biting.

"Hm, well, I make no promises. I have no power, but I will try my best."

"That's all we can ask," Nash said.

With that, they finally left, and only then did I head inside. So much for my project. I had hoped to create a special for the day. I had been thinking about something with salmon. Now I didn't have time as I'd need to get right to work on today's menu and the soup of the day.

I headed inside and got right to work. First, checking the inventory, marking what things I would need Noah and Cullen to order for us. After that, I started cooking. The soups took the longest to cook, so I always started with those.

By the time Noah came in, I had all the soups going and much of the rest of the prep done. I was powered by pure frustration and anger, so much so, I could have probably run the entire restaurant alone today.

Watch out.

"Morning, Chef. How is Shayla?" Noah said, breaking my focus.

"She seems okay. In good spirits this morning when I left."

"Oh, good," he said with a smile. "I'm glad she was comfortable going to you."

"I know. I'm happy she was, too." I frowned, trying not to think of the worst-case scenario for her. "Oh, hey, has Marco seemed really off to you? Have people been talking about him?"

"Yeah, he has really gone downhill since we last talked about him." He ran a hand through his hair. His face fell. "I'm really worried about the guy."

"Me too. I really need to figure this murder out."

Noah's phone chimed.

"Speak of the devil. He has to take today off. Needs to meet with his lawyer again or something."

"Ugh, we need to hire a few more people, don't we?"

We were down by two people. Shayla and Marco. We could miss Shayla as we had enough kitchen staff, but Marco would be harder to replace with our current staff. We needed more front staff like servers and bussers.

"I'm on it." He jogged off to the office.

"Hey, wait," I said. He paused. "I had a run in this morning with some protesters out front."

"Really? Protesting the restaurant?"

"No, no. The Jamison Heights Complex project." I could feel my anger ramping up again just thinking about them.

"Here? Why?"

"Because I've gone out with Todd a few times."

"Oh, really? Jess, look at you dating. I didn't think you did that."

"You set me up once."

"You're right, I did, but that took forever and, well, it didn't end well."

"Sadly, no."

His friend, Colt, had been shot on his way to meet me for our first date. It wasn't related to me, but I still felt guilt. Thankfully, I had found his murderer and shone a light on embezzlement at the high school.

"So, how did you get them to leave?" he asked.

"I told them I would talk to Todd."

"Are you really going to talk him out of the project?"

I thought for a moment. It didn't make sense to talk him out of it. I gained nothing either way, so I really didn't have skin in the game. I had just wanted them to leave. Plus, as much as I loved the idea of a park, I was in favor of the new development. It would be good for my business.

"No, not at all, but I will at least talk to him."

Noah nodded. "Well, I'll get started on finding us some new employees."

"Thanks!"

I got back to work, trying not to think about Piper and her smirky face. That face. I wanted to smack that smug look right off it.

Deep breaths. Deep breaths.

An hour and a half into service, there was shouting in the dining room. Ava came running back.

"There are protesters in the dining room."

"Did anyone call the police?" I asked her.

"Yes, and Noah is trying to get them out now, but he wanted me to tell you what was happening."

I thought they were going to leave me alone. I looked over at Hannah, she nodded. We had an understanding that when I had to step away, she would watch my station. However, with protesters in the dining room, I didn't expect any new orders while I was dealing with that.

I dried my hands, no time to wash them completely as I made my way to the dining room. It was pure chaos as the protesters were marching around the tables, chanting about the building.

Looking around, as I tried to figure out where to start, I saw my staff trying to gain control of the situation and keep our customers calm and safe. I did a quick employee headcount.

Good. Looks like they are all here.

Scanning further, my eyes locked with Piper as her classic smirk spread across her face as she continued chanting.

"Park, not a building. Park, not a building!"

"Hey, hey, I thought y'all were over this. I called Todd like you said."

"But did you talk to him?"

"No, I have been working. I have a business to run."

"Well, here we are." She let out an evil laugh as she went back to her chant.

"No, you need to get out. You can't do this inside. You can move it out to the public streets, but not inside a private business."

"I don't think so."

I stood in her way. She pushed me. Since she was nearly a foot shorter than me and maybe fifty pounds lighter, I didn't move much. She tried again, but again, I stood my ground. She growled and snarled, coming at me once more. I couldn't help but picture a rabid badger. It almost made me giggle.

The more I dodged, didn't engage, and never fell over, the angrier she got. But there was no way I was going to participate in a fight with her. It would get me nowhere.

"That's enough!" A stern voice said.

We all turned to see that the police had arrived. The voice belonged to Officer Kyle Rafferty. He caught my eyes and gave me a slight smile before turning back to the crowd, his face stern again.

"If you are not an employee or a customer, please step outside," he said.

"We have a right to protest!" Nash yelled.

"You can do it on the street, in a public space, but not inside a private business," Raff said. "Now, out or you are all being taken in."

They grumbled but started to funnel out. Piper gave me a once over before she stomped her way out. Officers Roberts and Wright followed them out, while Rafferty stayed behind.

"You good?" Raff asked.

"Yeah, I just need to check on my customers and employees." I looked around. My staff was already checking on all the tables. "Thank you for coming so quickly."

"Of course. Always there for my friend." He nodded. "You sure you're okay?"

"Yes, she didn't touch me. She tried, but—" I shrugged.

"You're awesome. Let me know if you need anything." He patted my arm.

After Raff left, I made my rounds through the dining room to check on each table. Nobody seemed upset with us and were very understanding of the situation.

"You handled that so well, Chef."

"Those people are crazy."

"We have seen them all over town."

"Don't worry about a thing, Chef. The town loves you."

I thanked each and every person, including touching base with as many employees as I could. They were a little shaken up, but overall okay. We'd some crazy things happen since we'd opened, but this one was at the top of my list as the worst, since it happened with customers in the dining room.

I was ready to pat myself on the back for a crisis averted, when at the last table, I noticed Kay the socially awkward member of Todd's team with the strange mood swings.

"Hi, Kay. I want to apologize for the disruption."

"Hey, Chef, no problem. It was like dinner and a show." She laughed.

"Well, I appreciate your patronage of my restaurant and your patience with the situation. I hope you enjoyed your meal."

"I did. I had the Reuben sandwich. Divine."

"Well, it was good to see you. I need to get back to the kitchen."

"Take care," she said. I turned, heading straight to the kitchen. I fought the urge to look back at her, but I had to act natural.

Why was she here? Was she involved with the protesters? Again, I had to question my own passions. Was I too passive about life? I had nothing I was that passionate about.

"That was crazy," I said to Noah once we were both in the kitchen.

"I have never seen anything so crazy. So, they *really* wanted you to talk to Todd?"

"I left him a voicemail. What more do they want?"

We shrugged in unison.

With that, we got back to work. I knew I was going to have to call a staff meeting to address this with all the employees and give them a few talking points if they ran into these people again. I might even get some advice from the police department about what we can and should do if they returned.

Obviously, I didn't handle it well by antagonizing Piper. It wasn't intentional, but still, I had. I wanted to avoid that next time. For that matter, I wanted to avoid a next time.

The evening shift showed up. News had already reached them from the online gossip channels.

"I heard y'all had a big hullabaloo here this afternoon," June said, coming in to take over for me.

"You could say that."

"Do you think they'll come back?"

"Rafferty messaged me that they all got ticketed, so no, I don't think so."

"Okay, good. He's a good egg."

I smiled at her, before stepping away from the station to wash my hands, then headed to the office.

"I think we might need to have a staff meeting in the next few days," I said to Noah and Cullen. They were both in the office doing their evening turnover.

They both looked at me. Noah's shoulders dropped.

"Yeah, you're right."

"I can set it up for next week since it's Friday."

"Oh, yeah, true. Shoot for Tuesday, please."

"You got it." Cullen made a note.

I grabbed my purse to head out.

"Tell Shayla we miss her," Cullen called out. He worked in the evening when she usually worked.

"I'll tell her."

I stepped out the back door when my phone rang. It was my Auntie Rita.

"Hey, Auntie Rita. What's up?"

"Jessie, did you hear about Marco?" There was a slight waver in her voice, causing my blood to run cold. I had wanted to talk to her about him anyway, but clearly something other than a separation from his wife was wrong right now.

"No, what's going on?"

"He tried to commit suicide. They have him in the hospital."

"Ohmygosh. That's awful. I knew he had been spiraling, but I didn't know how bad it had gotten."

The back door of the restaurant opened, and Noah walked out of it. I gestured for him to stop. He waited, giving me an odd look as he started to listen to my conversation.

"Marta says he should be okay, but it will be a long road."

"Can he have visitors?"

"Not at the moment. They aren't even allowing the family in yet."

"Okay, will you let me know if you hear anything new?"

"Of course."

I hung up with my aunt, then turned slowly towards my friend and assistant manager.

"Marco tried to commit suicide this afternoon."

"He did what? Is he okay?"

"He is okay, but that's all I know. No visitors."

"Wow, things have really gotten out of control, huh?"

"Yeah, protesters in the restaurant. Marco charged with murder. Shayla beaten by her stepfather. I just wanted a boring restaurant."

"Yeah, we've had nothing but craziness since we opened. Time for a break." He fidgeted with his keys. "You okay?"

"Oh, yeah, I'm okay. You?"

"Yeah. Do you need anything for Shayla?"

"No, Vee has been home with her today, so I'm sure they have been doing nothing but watching movies."

"That sounds fun." He clicked his key fob, unlocking his car. "I'm heading over to April's."

"Oh, yeah? Tell April hey from me."

"I will." He smiled. "Well, see ya tomorrow."

"See ya."

As I drove home, my phone rang. I cringed before I looked at the display. It was Todd this time. I heaved a sigh of relief. I didn't want any more bad news today.

"Hey, Todd."

"Hey, beautiful." I was not used to being called beautiful. Each time he said it, my hands got clammy and my face warmed. I was thankful this conversation was over the phone.

"I guess you got my message from earlier today?"

"Yeah, and sorry, I'm only just now getting back to you. We have been redoing the blueprints and project timeline now that all the damage has been assessed. We have the funding, so I know what we can afford with the build. I have to cut some of the fixtures slightly, but it will still be nice."

"Oh, I'm sure it will be."

"So, what's up? You sounded off."

"I had the Dashwood Beautification Organization folks at my door this morning and they wanted me to call you."

"They did?"

"Yeah, they were threatening me if I didn't talk to you about stopping the project."

"Wow, they have some nerve."

"Well, the story gets better. They came back at around twelve-thirty and protested all through my restaurant, shouting and chanting. I had customers at the time."

"Oh hell. I'm sorry. This has gotten out of hand, but I told you that group is trouble. They will do anything to stop this project. *Anything*."

"I'm getting the idea."

"Did they cause any damage or hurt anyone?"

"No, and the customers were all understanding. I think some of them enjoyed the drama of it. Nothing like that happens in Dashwood, at least not normally."

"Ha, yeah, I bet." He chuckled. "So, hey, the other reason I was calling, I wanted to see if you were free tomorrow night. I'm thinking dinner and a movie."

"Um, yeah, I'd like that."

"Great! I'll pick you up around six tomorrow."

"Sounds good."

With that, we chatted a little more, but I arrived at home, so we got off the phone. I sat in the car for a moment, thinking about all the insanity of the day. Protesters, suicide, and a date. It was unbelievable.

Chapter Thirteen

Thankfully, Saturday at work was uneventful. No protesters. No unexpected visitors.

Plus, Auntie Rita relayed a message from Marta Reyes about Marco. He was recovering well, and on Monday, he would be transferred to the VA Hospital in Pinehurst for inpatient treatment.

Of course, I understood, and he would always have a job here once he returned, but we needed to move forward with hiring. Noah had already started the process. Thank goodness for me, Noah said he could handle it all. It was my least favorite part of the job.

If I didn't have Noah, though, I know I would have to do it. I hadn't yet built that relationship with Cullen.

I was sitting in the office, waiting for Noah to be done in the dining room. He was talking with a customer. Cullen hadn't come in yet, so it was just me thinking.

I started slowly spinning in the office chair and talking to myself.

"If only I could hack into those cameras, I could see what happened." I groaned. "I need a computer person."

"I can do that, Chef," a voice said.

I stopped spinning and saw that Cullen had come in while I was musing.

"You can hack into a security camera? I thought you just did spreadsheets and social media."

"Everyone has a hobby." He chuckled, sliding his backpack from his back and pulling out an interesting-looking computer. "This baby here is my homemade beauty. She can hack into the Pentagon. Not that I have ever tried, mind you, but I'm sure I could if I wanted to."

Knowing he built it himself, the mismatched look made sense. It looked like Franken-computer, or pieces of other laptops mashed together.

"Well, I don't need that level of hacking, but good to know."

"Okay, so where are these cameras that you need? I'm assuming this has to do with Marco and the Jamison Heights Complex stuff."

"Yep, but the ones I need are on Greer. Though they might not have power or monitoring. Does that change your … um … ability?"

"No problem. If they are plugged in, they have power. Monitoring doesn't matter to me."

His computer whirled to life and the dark screen with a skull as the wallpaper blazed. A pop-up window with a neon blue cursor appeared. He began typing various symbols and characters.

"Can you read that?" He winked.

"Nope, I mean, I can see that's an ampersand, and that's the number three, but I just have to assume you know what you are doing."

He laughed. "Yep, I got this."

He continued typing, mumbling every once in a while, and then a video screen popped up. I immediately recognized it as across the street from where I had been parked just days ago. It was facing the building behind the Jamison Heights one, the old Sloane Department store building, and we had a clear view of the entrance leading down the alley.

"This is it! Wow, Cullen, you are a genius."

"That's what my resume says."

"Well, I know you are joking, but it really should."

"What should?" Noah asked, coming in. "What is that piece of junk?"

"My computer." Cullen chuckled.

"And what have you done here?"

"We accessed the Greer Street cameras."

"Nice. I didn't know you could do that. I thought you just did social media stuff." Noah chuckled.

"Why does everyone think that I'm so one dimensional?" Cullen asked.

"You are just so quiet," I said. "So, do you think you can back it up to the day of the fire?"

"Let me try." He started typing in the weird code again. It was a few minutes of him typing and muttering before he threw in the towel. "I can probably do it, but I need a bit more time and my home network. Our Wi-Fi here doesn't have enough speed."

"Okay, thanks for at least getting us this far," I said, pushing back.

Noah and I went through our business, just boilerplate stuff.

"And I saw the staff meeting on the schedule. Thank you for that," I commented.

"Yep, we need to discuss Marco and the protesters, and then I want to remind them about the holidays coming up. We'll need their requests for time-off."

"Yes. Thank you for thinking of that." I looked at the notes I'd made. "Have we had many applications for the busser and server positions?"

"Yes, I think we'll have plenty of good applicants and I've already started to set up interviews."

"Great. Well, I think that's it from me."

"Me too. Heading out?"

"Yep."

With that, we said good night to Cullen, then went our separate ways.

Having gotten at least a step closer to a clue, I sighed a nice cleansing breath in and out. I wanted to leave work with a clear mind and could simply focus on my date tonight. Todd was picking me up around six, so I wanted to shower and have time to unwind a bit.

When I pulled up at home, I saw the new people going into their house. They had their hands full of groceries and their backs turned as they scampered rapidly into their unit. I had my arm poised to wave, but they never turned once.

Strange.

They had been quiet neighbors so far. Although, technically, they lived across from us.

Sawyer had yet to get any good intel on them. Even Barb and Sandy, in 1408, hadn't gotten us anything either. If even they couldn't get it, there might not be anything interesting. Just boring people, living an ordinary life, like we are.

I couldn't help being a little paranoid about new people with all the strange things that had been happening around me the past six or seven months. I seemed to look for problems now, even where there weren't any.

I jogged up the couple of steps.

"Hello," I yelled.

I was greeted with a chorus of shouts, and Vee came running to hug me.

"How was work?" she asked, after letting me go.

"Busy, no crazy events. Perfect."

"Just like we like it," Shayla said. She came in holding Lulu. They had become fast friends.

I gave my cat's head a scratch.

"Did you hear anything from your mother?"

She frowned. "No, but I don't expect to either. She cares more for that man she is married to than her own daughter."

"Any idea if he ever made bail?"

"Officer Perez called earlier to check in and said no, they weren't able to get a bond yet."

"Well, that's good, yes?"

"I guess." A mix of emotions played across her face. I could understand. Blended families could be difficult, even in good situations. My family sure had a weird dynamic, but at least Samuel wasn't abusive.

"Did I miss anything exciting around here today?"

"We're looking at the clues all day," Vee said.

"Oh, yeah? Figure anything out?"

I had added Kimberly, Piper, Nash, and the Dashwood Beautification Organization to the clue board.

"Not yet, but we moved things around a bit and then back. It was just a brainstorming exercise," she said.

"But I find this all super exciting! I have never been part of a murder investigation before," Shayla said.

I'm glad it was providing her with a little distraction. Anything to keep her mind busy. That was the plan. Don't let her slow down long enough to think about her home life.

Maybe I shouldn't have made plans to go out tonight. I had worked both yesterday and today, which left her to my roommates. I hated to burden them.

Though neither seemed bothered. Vee had taken a liking to her and Sawyer had messaged me that she was good at his favorite zombie game.

S: **She keeps beating everyone. She's a great teammate**

Me: **Good**

S: **Where has she been my whole life? Well, video game life…**

Me: **Ha. Glad you are enjoying having a little sister**

I looked at them all now. They were smiling and seemed in good spirits. Not put out by being stuck together while I lived life, but I still felt some guilt.

"Are y'all sure you're okay with me going out tonight?"

"Of course!"

"Yes!"

"How will we ever find out if this guy is the killer if you don't?" Shayla laughed.

I couldn't help but join her in laughing at that, too. It was true. We still hadn't ruled him out. So why was I still going out with him? I mentally slapped myself.

"If y'all are sure?"

"We're sure!" They all said in near unison.

"Okay, okay. Let me go shower." I laughed. "Do y'all have a plan for dinner or do you need me to cook before I go?"

"I got it, Chef … er, I mean, Jess," Shayla said.

"I like having two chefs in the house," Sawyer said, rubbing his hands together. "Lots of good meals."

"It's the least I can do, plus it makes me happy to cook." Shayla smiled, putting the cat down. Lulu had started to wiggle and push to get down. She didn't like being held long.

"Well, good." I went upstairs to shower and dress.

I took my time enjoying the water running over me. I hadn't realized how sore I was from the day until I got into the shower. Hopefully, this didn't ruin the evening. I didn't want to be a downer.

After I got out, I dressed in my black Trash Pandas band shirt. It had a steampunk racoon playing a drum set that was made from trash cans. I paired that with my gray peasant skirt and black ankle boots with the chunky heels. I loved this outfit. I twirled the full skirt a bit as I took in the full view in the mirror.

"Perfect."

I headed downstairs as the smell of onions, tomatoes, and oregano floated up. Shayla must be making something Italian. I was a bit jealous. She made fantastic spaghetti and meatballs, and that's exactly what it smelled like.

"Whatcha got cooking in here?"

"I think you know, Jess." Shayla giggled.

"It smells so good. I'm a little jealous. Can I taste?"

"Of course." She handed me a spoon.

"Oh, my gosh, this is so good. I think you've outdone yourself with this one."

"Really? You think?"

"Oh, yes. Excellent."

"Did I hear we are in for a treat tonight?" Sawyer said, coming in.

"Of course you heard something about food." I laughed.

"Hey, I like food. What can I say?"

"But it's not fair you stay as thin as a rail. I even think about food, and I gain another five pounds," Vee said. Poor thing was at least fifty pounds overweight. She tried to work out and eat right, but she couldn't lose weight. While my mother had always described me as big-boned, I wasn't exactly overweight. I was just a large person.

I gave her a side hug of support. She smiled at me.

There was a knock at the door. Vee giggled.

"Your date's here."

"Hush," I whispered. "Do I look okay?"

"Yes."

"Love the Trash Pandas tee!"

"That skirt is perfect."

I smiled at them. It was the confidence I needed at that moment.

"Okay, wish me luck."

I turned to answer the door as he knocked again. Opening the door, he looked up with a bright smile.

"Hey, Jess. Wow, you look great." He put his hand on his heart. He was in a black and gray bowling shirt with black slacks and black and gray tennis shoes.

"So do you." I smiled, stepping out. "Ready?"

"Yep." He put his arm out. I linked mine with his to walk to his car.

Once I was seated in the passenger side, I watched him jog around to his side of the car. I said a silent prayer, hoping to settle this whole thing with my doubts about him tonight. Either I would continue to date him and just determine he was not the killer, or I would end things because I suspected he was the killer.

"Alrighty, I was thinking about going to Spicy Fig Bistro. Have you been there yet?"

"Only takeout, but not at the restaurant. It was really good."

"Well, great."

We headed that way.

"So, how is the project going?" I asked.

"It looks like we will likely get our approvals we need to move forward, despite the delays caused by *that organization*."

"You still think they are the arsonists?"

"I do."

I nodded slightly. His overconfidence about it had me having doubts about him. I really needed to make my mind up on this, but I didn't feel like I had enough information.

Bleep! This one was hard.

We parked and walked into the new restaurant. It was roughly 70 seats, if my estimate was right, so on the smaller side, but it was perfect. Minimalist decor which wasn't my style, but in certain places, it felt right.

I liked artwork, plants, and something showing personality. This was a blank slate.

The walls here were broken up by a chair rail at about three foot high. From the floor to the railing was a shiny cherry wood and then from the rail to ceiling was painted black. There was a mirror on one side and a window on the other. Then the whole back wall was the kitchen and bathrooms. They had an open kitchen, so you could see the staff cooking.

There were only three other tables with customers, but I could see the to-go counter was packed with orders. I guess they did a lot of takeout orders. Made sense, because that's what we had previously done.

"For two?" The host greeted us with a smile.

"Yes."

We followed him to a table against the wall near the front window. It had a nice view of city hall.

"Your server will be right with you."

We skimmed over the menu, making small talk. Our server took our drink order and brought us some pita, hummus, and some olives. It was a yummy little treat.

After we ordered, we continued to make small talk, mostly talking about what movie to see after.

"There is that new action one," I suggested.

"I thought you might be into the comedy with what's his name?"

"Gates Landing?"

"Yeah, that one."

"It looks like a Rom-Com. Are you into that?" I asked.

"I mean, why not? I'm not completely insensitive." He softly chuckled.

"Alrighty, then Gates Landing."

A moment later, the server brought our food. I had gotten the falafel platter. It had three falafels on it, along with a tzatziki sauce, a cucumber and tomato salad, pickled onions, and some pitas.

"This looks so good," I said to the server. He looked surprised but smiled and nodded.

He then set Todd's gyro platter down and scurried away.

"Not much of a people person, is he?" Todd teased. "But this does look good. I might have a little plate envy." He eyed my plate a little.

"Well, you'll have to remember this for next time, huh?" I said, as I scooped some of the cucumber salad into my mouth.

"That's mean," he laughed, but then picked up his gyro and began eating.

Halfway through our meal, his phone chimed. He picked it up.

"Oh, shi#, um, shoot. I need to call the police. Excuse me."

"Wait, what happened?"

He flashed me the screen. It was from an unknown number and said if he didn't stop the project, he would be *hunted down and quartered*.

"Yikes! Yeah, call."

I sat there with my hands in my lap as I listened to his side of the call. At least I knew he was likely not the killer, unless he had staged this to take the target off of himself. Maybe he had a friend send him a text. I decided to give him the benefit of the doubt, for now, as that seemed really unlikely.

"Okay. Yes. Unknown. Maybe. Okay, let us just finish our meal and pay, then I'll head that way to make the report. Thank you." He ended the call and then looked at me. "I need to call our date short to go make a police report. I'm so sorry."

"No, I'm sorry that you have to deal with this."

"Thanks. These people are crazy."

We ate in mostly silence after that, the joy sucked out of our date. Once we were done eating, we settled the bill, then headed out to his car.

"Do you want me to go to the station with you, or would it be easier if I got a ride home?"

"Um, I don't know." His face had lost all color after he got that text. "I can't think straight."

"Why don't I come with you for support, okay?"

He simply nodded.

"Do you want me to drive?"

"Okay."

He handed me the keys, and we both climbed in. I drove us to the police station just a few blocks away. I tried to distract him, but he was just staring out the window.

"Why me?" he muttered as we pulled into the police station.

"Honestly, I have been asking myself that same question since I was five years old."

"What?"

"My father killed a man in front of me when I was five." I parked in one of the visitor spots and turned to face him.

"Holy ... Wow!" That broke some of the stress. A bit of color came back to his face. "So, this stuff isn't exactly new to you?"

"I mean, no, but I haven't really had to deal with it much since then."

He studied my face, a slow, cautious smile forming on his face.

"Okay, I'm back. Sorry, I checked out for a minute or ten. Thank you." He touched my hand. "Let's get this over with."

An hour later, we were walking out of the station after he gave all the information he had, which wasn't much. They couldn't trace the text message but would try to work with the phone company.

"But to be honest, unless this person gives us a clue, we just have limited resources in our department." Officer Dorian said.

It wasn't something I hadn't heard from others. I didn't know Officer Dorian well. He worked mostly in the office. He was an older officer and my theory was that he wasn't as fast as the others. Though I had no proof, that was why he stayed behind.

Back in his car, Todd looked at me.

"Sorry our date was a bust, but I do appreciate you standing by me for this."

"Of course. I was happy to help."

We headed back to my house, and after a kiss good night, our third date was over. I had officially taken him off of my suspect list, even though there was still a small possibility that he had the message sent to throw me off. I just gave him the benefit of the doubt.

Chapter Fourteen

I laid in bed the next morning, not wanting to get up yet. It had been another fitful night with anxiety-filled tossing and turning. I really hoped Cullen could come through with some solid footage so I could clear Marco, and we could be done with this business.

Last night, after my date, Vee, Shayla, and I stood in front of the clue board for an hour, talking out everything we had listed, which still wasn't much. It was mostly just names, motives, and a few objects.

We'd added the death threat, but without a suspect linked, that was almost useless.

"Who could it be?"

"I would bet it's Piper and Nash," Shayla said.

"My money is on Foster," Vee said.

"Okay, I need to hear reasons." I pointed first to Shayla.

"Well, they just seem so sus, don't they? They were super violent at the restaurant. They have been running all over town shouting about Todd and protesting this project."

"Yeah, they do seem angry all the time, especially Piper," Vee said. "It could be she just has a crush on him and she's mad that he is interested in Jess."

"What? No, why would she be jealous of me?"

"Look at you. You're gorgeous."

"You look beautiful. Almost glowing."

"Y'all are making me blush." I tried to brush it off.

They exchanged a giggle.

"Okay, back to the board. Why do you think Foster?"

"His creepy questions to you. How he is just randomly around."

She had a point. Heck, they both had points. But creepy and potentially jealous, didn't mean they murdered an innocent man, right?

"I need Cullen to come through for me," I mumbled.

"That's so cool he can do that. I just thought he was a big ole nerd." Shayla laughed.

"I thought so, too, but no, he has some super computer skills."

"I always thought he was kinda cute," Vee said, dreamily.

"Cullen?" Shayla and I both asked.

"Yeah, y'all don't think so?" Vee pouted.

"There is a key for every lock," I said.

"Why are you so old?" Vee teased.

Needless to say, after that we got way off topic and didn't solve a thing. But it had at least given me some things to ponder.

I had today off and the four of us were going hiking at our favorite spot. It always gave me clarity of mind walking along the wooded path, listening to the birds, feeling the breeze on my face.

Lulu jumped from the bed, circling my legs.

"You want some food?"

She meowed up at me, so I filled her bowl, then I headed downstairs for coffee. Lulu ran ahead of me and straight to Shayla's room. I could hear her pawing at the door. A moment later, it creaked open and Lulu disappeared inside.

I chuckled quietly as I waited for the coffee. Lulu had really taken to Shayla, but still slept with me most nights. I think Shayla liked her just as much.

With my coffee in hand, I went to stare into the refrigerator. *Breakfast, breakfast,* I thought.

"Good morning," Vee said, coming into the room. "What's on the menu?"

"No idea yet."

"I vote for your awesome waffles," Sawyer announced, coming in with a yawn.

"With that good sausage."

"I can do that." I started grabbing ingredients and whipping up a big batch of waffles.

As the waffle batter rested, I made the sausage patties. It was a special sausage mix that I ground myself. We didn't offer breakfast at The Crock pot, but if we did, I would add this to the menu.

The smell of food must have crept into the spare room, because as the sausage was happily frying in the pan, the door opened.

"It always smells so good here," Shayla said, coming out. She helped herself to some orange juice, then sat next to Vee at the kitchen island. Vee gave her a soft hug.

"How are you feeling today?" Vee asked.

"Hm, still a little sore, of course, but I think the eye looks better." She pointed at it. "What do you think?"

Vee examined it. "Yeah, I think it's looking better."

"Do you think you can hike with us today?" I asked.

"Oh, yeah, for sure."

"Great."

I finished cooking, and everyone filled up on carbs, sugar, and the fatty protein of the sausage.

"This was so good, Jess. Thank you," Shayla said. "I'm getting spoiled quickly here."

"We're so glad." Vee giggled. "I love having a little sister."

Shayla smiled at her. They had really bonded over the few days that Shayla had been here. Tomorrow will be the first normal day for all of us. Shayla would return to school and work, and the rest of us to work. Vee and Sawyer would drop her off at school and Mr. Jones said he would make sure she got to work.

"I'll clean up while you ladies start getting ready for the park," Sawyer said as he began picking up plates.

"Great!"

"You're the best."

"Awesome."

An hour later, we were dressed and heading out. As we were getting in the car, movement across the street had me looking over. A person started to come out, cursed and backed up quickly.

"Did you see that?" I asked.

"No, what?" Vee asked, looking around.

"The neighbor across the street." I climbed in. "They started to come out and then hurried back inside. They looked like … Nash."

"The guy from the beautification thing?" Shayla asked, turning in the seat to look.

"Yeah, I think so. It looked like him, but I didn't get a good look."

"But why would he do that?"

"I don't know." I eyed the unit carefully as we drove away. A curtain moved in the upstairs window as we turned, and the building was no longer visible.

I tried to put it out of my mind as we arrived at the park. It was the perfect fall day for a walk through the woods. A bit overcast with low humidity and nothing but two miles of nearly empty trail ahead of us.

I stretched as I got out of the car, breathing out any negative energy.

"It's a good day," Vee chirped as she bounced towards the trail head.

We took our time, enjoying the weather and the sights. About an hour later, we were back at the car. It was an uneventful, relaxing break from life, and more specifically, the murder investigation.

Now I had to get my mind right for Sunday dinner. I knew the topic of Marco and what I was doing to solve the murder would come up.

When we parked in front of our townhouse, I was tempted to run across the street. If Nash was living there, I wanted to know why. I chickened out and went inside with the rest of my group. It would have to wait.

While we were relaxing, I saw that I had an email from Cullen with a file attached. It was the footage from the day of the fire. He said it was grainy, but he was calling in a favor from a buddy who should be able to clean it up.

But it will take a few days, His note said. It also said that he cut out some of the dead time, only including the action parts. The time frame between them going down the alley to when they reappeared was roughly twenty-eight minutes.

I hit play. I could see three figures emerge from the left screen, duck down the alley, and then the picture was only of the alley. Then it jumped to them running back to Greer Street and then back to where they started.

There was a weird light now coming from the alley, a fluttery, flickering light. Then headlights flashed as part of a car drove by, but it was difficult to see the full car or tell the color on the black and white screen. That's when the video ends.

"Look at this." I showed the others.

"Wow."

"It really is grainy."

"So, it really looks like three people."

"Yeah. Now I don't know what to think."

"We need to write this on the board, right? Isn't that what y'all would do next?" Shayla asked. "Can I write it?"

"Sure."

"Oh, yay!" She ran to the office and before we could join her, she was already writing 'three people on security footage.' She flashed it towards us.

"Looks good."

She tacked it up, then stepped back with a huge grin on her face. I am so glad she was here with us. At least it was another clue, even if it wasn't enough to solve this yet. We now knew there were three people involved.

Once Cullen had a clearer video, we would know who it was, I hoped.

~ ~

We pulled up at Granny Ines and Auntie Rita's right on time. There was a car in the driveway that I didn't recognize.

"Who's car is that?"

"No idea, but you know they often invite people from church."

"True."

We climbed out of the car. I knocked as I opened the door.

"Hello. Granny, Auntie," I called out.

"Back here!" Auntie Rita called.

We followed her voice to the kitchen. Normally, we sat in the living room, visiting before dinner, so this was weird. As we came into the room, I saw who the car belonged to. It was Marta and Selene Reyes. Marco's mother and his wife. I had only met them a few times.

"You know our guests. This is Marta and this is Selene."

"Hi, yes, we've met a few times. How are you?"

"Nice to see you, Chef," Marta said with a smile.

Selene simply smiled.

"We were just finishing preparing dinner and visiting," Granny said.

"What's on the menu for today?" Sawyer asked, going to hug both Granny and Auntie Rita.

"We thought we would have picadillo, tacos, and elote."

"Yum. I love it."

"It will be just a few minutes more."

"How is Marco doing?" I asked Marta and Selene. Selene sucked in a breath.

"He's doing okay," Marta said, taking Selene's hand. "It was scary for sure, but we are so glad that she found him before … well, just before."

"We're all praying for him and you both." I said.

"Thank you. It truly means a lot to us," Marta said.

"Once he is settled in the VA Hospital, I will call you to come visit him," Selene said. "I know it would lift his spirits to have a visit from you."

"I would really like that." I reached for her hand, giving it a light squeeze. "And if you need anything, we are here for you. Not just as church friends, but as The Crock Pot family."

Selene made a sound, but no words came out.

Marta spoke for her. "That truly means a lot."

"Well, that is enough sad talk," Granny said. "Let's eat some nice comfort food and speak of cheerful things, like the coming holidays."

I let the subject change, but I really wanted to tell them that we were close. I had security footage and just needed it to be cleaned up. Then we would know for sure.

I smiled at everyone as I listened to them talk about things other than murder or suicide. It ended up being a nice evening and as usual, we were sent away with a ton of leftovers.

As we were saying goodbye, Selene assured me she would reach out once she had a time for me to visit. I hugged her and wished her well.

"And if you need anything, anything, we are just a phone call away."

"Thanks so much, Jess. You are an amazing boss and person."

I liked to think so, I thought as we drove away.

Chapter Fifteen

Everyone was gathered around the bar area. We had no customers in the restaurant at the moment, but Jordan and Ava were prepared to jump up to assist if anyone came in.

"Okay, thanks for staying late or coming in early for this. I just wanted to address some of the recent issues, specifically the protesters. Kudos to the day staff for how well y'all handled things. Not stopping them was smart, just keeping the guests calm was perfect. We shouldn't see them back, but if we do, just call the police and stay calm is the best we can do. Any questions about that?"

"I'm sorry I missed it," Parker laughed.

"It was nuts!" Ripley said.

"I wanted to push them out or block the door, but I didn't know what to do. There were so many of them," Jordan said. She had been at the host stand when they arrived.

"You handled it well. I thought I was going to panic," Skye added.

"You all did well. Thank you all. Now, I have an update on Marco. I saw his mother and wife the other day, and he is stable, getting the help he needs. I will be going to visit him on Wednesday and can give another update then."

"Tell him we miss him!"

"Tell him we're thinking about him."

"Wish him the best from us."

"I will give him all the messages. I'm sure he will appreciate them." I smiled. "Last bit of business. Holidays are coming. We will be open on Thanksgiving Day, but not on Christmas day or New Year's day. So, we need to make schedules early. Submit your requests and we will try to accommodate as best we can. Any questions?"

"Are we allowed to dress up for Halloween?"

"Um, I hadn't thought about it yet, but as long as it meets health code, I don't see why not. Noah, thoughts?"

"Yeah, like Chef said, as long as it doesn't violate health code, let's do it."

There were cheers and high-fives.

"Any other questions?" I looked around. Nobody had any. "Alrighty, that's a wrap."

With that, the group broke up. Day shift transitioned to the evening shift, and I went to the office to talk to Cullen.

"Any news on the security footage from your friend?"

"Not yet, but he has it. I'm hoping any day now."

"Okay, let me know as soon as you can. That footage is the key."

"I will."

"Well, I guess I'll head home. Night."

With everything done, I headed home. When I arrived, I noticed someone standing across the street. They turned. It was Foster.

Panic flashed over his face as he started to go left then right, like you see a squirrel do when it gets caught in the street, but then they just kind of freeze. Yeah, Foster was just standing wide eyed.

"Um, hi," he said, as I exited my car.

"Hi. What are you doing here? Visiting Nash?" I took a chance, since I actually wasn't sure if Nash did live there. It was just a hunch.

He looked over his shoulder at the unit. "Who?" His voice cracked.

"Nash ... um, I'm blanking on his last name, but he is part of the Dashwood Beautification Organization. The ones protesting the project you are part of."

"Oh, right, that Nash." He coughed. "Yeah, I was dropping off a memo from Todd. You can ask him. It is a cease-and-desist letter."

"So, why so squirrely about it?" I would have laughed at my joke, but he wouldn't have understood.

"I wasn't expecting to see you is all. Do you live around here?" He gestured.

"I do." But somehow, I believe he already knew that.

He gave me a once over. "I still don't know what Todd sees in you. He isn't the man you think he is."

My mouth fell open. I guess he gained his composure

"What is your problem with me? I have done nothing to you."

"You're just too nosy for your own good. Keep digging on Todd, though. I am sure you will find what you are looking for." With that, he took off at a fast walk, turning the corner without a look back. I heard a car start, then a green sedan drove by on the cross street.

Why do people keep leaving before finishing a conversation? I guess from their point of view; they were done. I had lots of questions.

I stood there only a second more, trying to process what he said. "Keep digging on Todd." I mumbled it, then turned on my heel and headed straight inside to my computer.

Firing it up, I did a search for Todd Barber.

The results were what I had seen before with his city council profile, his social media, and past projects. There were some professional headshots and then a few casual pictures of him at ground breakings or city functions. Nothing crazy.

I sighed.

Maybe if I click to page two of the search results. The results here were a little mixed, and there were starting to be people with similar names showing. But still nothing unusual that would make me think Todd is a killer.

Then my eyes caught an article about lawsuits for using faulty or cheap materials, subpar work, and delays in meeting project deadline. The suit alleges that he pocketed the difference in material costs.

Okay, that was a wrong, but not killer level.

Until I found another lawsuit and another. Perhaps this was something to look at. An hour later, I was still sitting at the computer, and had yet to take a shower, when my roommates came home.

"Honey, we're home!" They yelled.

"Hey, you haven't showered yet? I thought we were going to Pins for bowling and dinner?" Vee said.

"Oh, bleep! I'm sorry. I got some juicy gossip." I relayed what happened with Foster and then all the information I found on Todd. "Look, I counted it is at least six different projects, so why would Mayor Lackland and the rest of the city council endorse him for this project?"

"Um, interesting. He lied, obviously, and then nobody checked."

"Obviously, but it just feels … I don't know. Something."

"Are you going to ask him about it?"

"I honestly don't know. We aren't … like, serious or anything. It was just a few dinners. Nothing serious."

"You kissed."

"Barely. More like pecks. Nothing I would count as anything profound or earth shattering."

"He is a weird dude." Sawyer said. "I'm going to change. I'm starving."

"Oh, bleep, let me go shower and get dressed. I just need five minutes, plus a few." I winked and raced up the stairs ahead of Sawyer.

I heard him laughing as he went into his room. I stripped and hit the shower. Twenty minutes, give or take later, I was joining my friends downstairs. We headed over to Pins Bowling Alley for some beer and pizza with a side of bowling.

We played three games and ate two large pizzas, taking our time with both.

"What time do we need to pick up Shayla?"

"Nine."

"Awesome. I have time for one of their ice cream sundaes." Vee said, jumping up and running to the counter.

"Did she even offer to get us one?" I asked Sawyer.

"No, no she did not." We laughed.

"So, what do you think I should do about Todd?"

"You want my opinion on this?"

"Yes, from both the point of view of a guy, but also one of my dearest friends."

"Alrighty. Ask him about it. As uncomfortable as it might be, you will not have peace until you do."

"I don't know how to start that conversation."

"Yeah, that part might be tricky, but you can do it." He kissed the top of my head as he stood to take his turn. He rolled the fourteen pound ball down the alley getting a strike. "Booyah!"

Vee came back with a tray loaded with three of Pins' famous ice cream sundaes. They were loaded with hot fudge, homemade whipped cream, chopped peanuts, colorful sprinkles and a cherry on top.

"This one is mine." She announced, grabbing the one with extra cherries.

I think Clark, the manager for Pins, had a little crush on her. Of course, he was older than her dad, so it wasn't more than him giving her a little extra of anything she wanted. Like fries or a few cherries on her sundae.

We ate our sundaes, watching the other bowlers play. Then it was time to pick up Shayla.

"Do we need to pick up something for her to eat?" Vee asked.

"I don't think so, but I can text her." I sent her a message. Her reply was almost immediate. "Okay, she says she's good."

Minutes later, we pulled into the back parking lot. I messaged her we were here. A moment later, the door open and a smiling Shayla came out.

"Hey, thanks for picking me up."

"No problem," Sawyer said.

"How was work? You feeling okay?"

"A little sore, but overall, I feel good. Work was busy. Tuesdays aren't usually that busy." She laughed.

"We like busy," I said. "Do you have any homework?"

"Um, yeah, a little, mom!" Shayla busted out into laughter. It was good to hear.

"Ha, yeah, who am I? At least I skipped all the newborn stuff."

Everyone laughed.

"I never thought I would see the day," Sawyer teased from the front.

"At the rate all three of us are going, none of us are going to have kids," I said.

"Dang, Jess. Jinx us all?" Sawyer laughed.

"I want kids," Vee said. "I just need to find a husband."

"You'll be a great mom," Shayla said, putting her hand on Vee. "We will find you a husband."

"Thanks, girl."

We turned onto our street.

"What is going on here?" Sawyer said.

There were cars on both sides of the street, police cars, and an ambulance. They seemed to be parked at Nash's unit, the formerly mysterious tenant. We couldn't even get down the street.

Sawyer had to back up and park on the cross street.

"I hope Nash is okay," I mumbled.

We walked quietly to our unit, but didn't go inside. All the residents were doing the same, standing outside of their units, watching and waiting to see what was happening. Between the dim lighting and the flashing lights, it was hard to see which police officers had responded or who else was standing across the street.

It was several minutes before the EMTs brought out a stretcher with a person on it. We couldn't see who it was because there was a sheet draped over them.

"Do you think that is Nash?" Vee whispered.

"Maybe."

There was a wailing sound coming from the house and a moment later, someone came running out towards the stretcher, grabbing at it. It looked vaguely like Piper.

"Nash! I'm sorry. I'm so sorry." She screamed out.

An officer tried to get her off the body. "Ma'am, get back. We need you to come back inside."

That sounded like Rafferty.

"I guess maybe we have another murder to solve," I whispered as we watched the ambulance drive away.

Slowly the other tenants started to go back into their units.

"I guess we should go in, too," I said. "Shayla needs to get her homework done and get some sleep before school tomorrow."

Three heads turned to stare at me.

"I heard it." I pouted as I opened our door.

Who am I? I thought.

Chapter Sixteen

After the excitement of last night, I didn't think I was going to be able to sleep, but I actually slept so well. I didn't even hear my alarm or my roommates when they left.

I hope Shayla got off to school okay.

I ignored my inner voice, who was teasing me for even thinking such motherly thoughts again.

Stretching, I headed downstairs for coffee, and I wanted to update our clue board. Nash was no longer a suspect, or at least one who could be charged.

With my coffee in hand, I went into the office, smiling when I saw how clean Shayla was keeping the room. She was such a sweet girl and a hard worker.

I took the piece of paper with Nash's name on it and wrote dead under his name, frowning as I stuck it back to the board. It was sad. I hadn't liked him, but that didn't mean I wished him dead.

"I just need that footage." I rubbed my head.

I had a gut feeling about who was involved, at least I did until Nash. I couldn't help but think those tools and wood were a bigger clue than I knew.

As much as I didn't want to, I added Todd back on the list with an exclamation point and added two on to Foster's name. It made sense. Nash was against them and their project. I caught Foster snooping yesterday. Was he trying to catch Nash? Had he succeeded?

"I should have checked our front door camera."

I pulled up the app on my phone and backed up the footage to yesterday afternoon to just before I saw my car pull up and me talking to Foster. From there, I ran the video at two times speed, until I saw the first police car roll up.

There was nothing leading up to that, but in all fairness, our camera was pointed mostly at our front door. It just caught the edge of that unit.

Foster had been standing barely in frame. I couldn't see what had happened to the left.

I groaned and gave up for now. I needed to get over to Pinehurst for my visit with Marco. They had told me to be there at ten. It was nearly nine now, and it was a thirty-minute drive, so I needed to get a move on.

Once I was dressed, I grabbed the gift bag with magazines and word puzzle books, then headed out the door. At the top of our steps, I looked across to Nash's unit. I hadn't known him well, but knowing he had died there made me sad.

Shaking off the sadness, I hopped in my car and headed towards Pinehurst. Thirty or so minutes later, I pulled into the parking lot of the VA

Hospital. It was a five story, brown brick building. Nothing unique or special about the building's appearance.

I walked through the front door and was amazed at the number of people milling about. I was just at Dashwood General Hospital with Shayla, and there weren't this many people. It took me a few moments to get my bearings and follow the signs to his room: third floor, west wing, room 376.

There was a nurse's desk as I got to the west wing.

"Hello, may I help you?" the nurse on duty asked.

"Yes, I am here to visit Marco Reyes. I'm Jessica Vasquez."

"Let me check." He typed into the computer. "Ah, yes, Jessica. I have you here. May I just check your driver's license or identification?"

I handed over my license with a smile. He looked at it and then me, smiling, then he handed it back.

"Alright, I have you checked in. He is straight down this hall," the nurse gestured to the left, "all the way at the end, last door on the right."

"Thank you so much."

I took a deep breath as I walked down the hallway. I wasn't sure why I was nervous. Perhaps because I didn't know what I was going to say to him.

Arriving at 376, I took another cleansing breath before knocking.

"Come in," A voice called. It didn't sound like Marco.

I pushed the door open slowly. I saw Marco sitting on the edge of his bed and next to him were his mother, Marta and his wife, Selene.

"Oh, I'm sorry. I didn't know you had visitors. Hi."

"No, it's okay. We were just leaving, Jessie," Marta said. She came over, hugging me. "I am so glad you are here." She whispered in my ear. "It will cheer him up a lot."

She let me go, turning to her son. "I'll be back this afternoon. Do you need anything?"

"No, I'm good." He smiled, softly. His voice was not as jovial and animated.

Marta kissed his head, then waved. Selene kissed him quickly, then followed her mother-in-law out. She smiled at me as she passed.

"I'm so sorry. I didn't mean to run them off. I thought they had told me to come at ten."

"No, you are right on time, Chef. Thank you for coming." He tried to smile, but it came out as a flat frown.

"I brought you some things." I handed him the bag.

"Thank you." He peeked in. "Oh, word puzzles. Love these."

"I remembered."

"I guess you have questions."

"No, not at all. Just here to support you and let you know I am here for you."

Tears formed in his eyes. "Like I told you before, I didn't kill Zach. I never would have. He was my friend, and I was trying to help him."

"I believe you."

"My mother and wife have doubts. I can see it in their eyes," he mumbled. "I have disappointed them."

"No, not at all. I had dinner with them on Sunday. Your mother is quite proud of you. She was bragging about your service."

"But I haven't done anything since then."

"You helped me get the restaurant going. That was extremely helpful to me. I couldn't have done it without you."

"While I appreciate that, I know you would have been just fine. You have a talent for surrounding yourself with talented, hard-working people."

"Like you." I gestured to him. I wanted to lecture him to take a compliment, but I knew he was struggling with life and demons right now.

He chuckled, softly. "I miss work. Ugh, I just need to get out of my head."

"Do you have any new ideas about who? Do you remember seeing anyone that night?"

He rubbed his head, then stood. "I have tried to replay it over and over in my head. I've told the police everything I can remember."

"Which way did you drive to the building?"

"Um, from the restaurant, I drove up West Street to Main and then over to Barker, passed Greer and turned right onto Jamison. I parked in front of the building, entering from the front."

When he said Greer, something clicked.

"Do you remember any vehicles or people on Greer?"

"Yeah, there was a … some kind of car, but it was kind of dark on Greer. That block has been a ghost town for so long." He paused. "Wait, you think whomever was in that car could have been the true killer?"

"Yes, I do."

"I wish I could remember more, but I wasn't thinking about it then. Damn, I'm usually more observant."

"That's okay. Cullen is working on the security footage."

"What do you mean, working on it?"

"He was able to … I guess hack into the security cameras and get the footage from that night."

"That's great! That will clear me, right?"

"It will as soon as we get a clean version of the video. It was kind of blurry, so he reached out to a friend to help."

"When will he have it?"

"I honestly don't know, but just know there is hope. We will fix this."

"Hot damn. This is the best news I've heard in days, weeks." He hopped up and grabbed me into a big bear hug. "Thank you, Chef!"

We made small talk for a few minutes after that. He was back to his joking, playful self by the time I left. I really hoped that Cullen's friend could come through with the clean footage, and it showed the people I thought it might.

Back in my car, I decided to send Todd a text. We needed to talk, and I needed it to be in a public, yet somewhat private place.

I knew just the spot.

Chapter Seventeen

I parked across the street from City Hall. Looking towards the memorial park, I could see Todd waiting. He checked his watch then looked around, but not in my direction.

Maybe I should have messaged Detective Upton, especially since I haven't talked to him in a while.

I shot off a quick message just telling him I was about to confront Todd about the murder of Zach. His reply was instant. I could almost feel his anger coming through the message.

U: **You are doing what?**

Me: **Confronting him about the murder**

U: **Where? What proof do you have?**

Me: **I don't want to tell you**

I didn't want to tell him the where or the what of this. So why had I reached out? I knew the answer. It was for my own safety and if Todd did confess, it would be good to have him close by.

U: **Jess**

Me: **Okay, but don't stop things. If you come, back-up only**

U: **Agreed**

Me: **The memorial park in front of city hall**

U: **You there now?**

Me: **Yes and he is waiting**

U: **Okay. I will park across the street and after you can explain**

Me: **Deal**

I put my phone on silent, took a deep breath, then exited my car. I really hoped Detective Upton didn't come disrupt things, but I felt better knowing he was on his way.

The air was still, hot, and thick as I walked across the street. It seemed like fitting weather for our conversation.

"Oh, hey, I was about to give up on you. Where did you park?"

"Just across the street. Easier for me to head home that way," I lied.

"Well, I'm happy to see you." He leaned over to kiss me. "Want to walk?"

"Yeah."

We walked through the garden. It wasn't as pretty as the last time I was here. The roses had old blossoms that were at the end of their life. Still, it was beautiful in design.

There were people milling around outside of the garden or going into city hall. It was in public, but nobody was close enough to overhear our conversation. Exactly the setting I wanted to have this discussion.

We didn't say anything until we walked all the way to the center.

"Want to sit?" He gestured.

"Yes." I let my eyes dart to the lot across the street. I saw Detective Upton pull in. It looked like he had a passenger. Who could that be? If I had to bet money, it would be Officer Kyle Rafferty, but I didn't know for sure.

"So, you wanted to talk?"

I didn't know exactly how to start this. Doing a mental shrug, I just went for it.

"I have been thinking about what Foster said."

"Which thing?" he chuckled.

I had to bite my tongue. I didn't find this funny the way he clearly did.

"The part about us dating, or you know, going on a few dates, anyway. He said it was only because of this investigation."

"Yes, so?"

"So? So? I don't date. I have had a string of bad luck in that arena. In fact, my most recent date was killed on his way to our first date." I exhaled. "And against my own inner voice telling me this was stupid, I let you charm me into not one, not two, but three dates. I let you kiss me, call me beautiful. I let my guard down. Then you sit there and ask me 'so,' when I want to know why you are interested in me."

Tears were threatening to fall, but after working in various kitchens since I was sixteen, I knew how to ignore and push them back. He was not worth the tears.

Todd just sat there with a blank expression on his face. I don't know if he was stunned by my admission or if he just didn't care. I had no intention of speaking again until after he responded to my statement.

"Look, I don't know what you want me to say. Are you interesting as a person? Yes. For that, yeah, I am interested in you, but we met because of the investigation. Plain and simple."

"So, you do want to keep dating me?"

He looked down at his shoes, mumbled a curse under his breath, then looked at me.

"I don't know what to say."

"You just answer the question."

"No, I guess, no. I don't."

"You were going to see this through until I solved this murder, which, by the way, I am close. That's the other reason I am here, but I will get to that."

"You solved it? Who is it?"

"Before I tell you, answer me, you were going to end things when I solved this, yes or no?"

"Probably."

"So, yes."

"Yes," He mumbled.

"Okay."

The tears and the lump in my throat disappeared. My mind was at ease. I knew now where we stood and exactly how I felt about him, too. I had had one foot out the door on this relationship from the beginning. Call it my own bad track record or insecurities or both. Either way I could now move on.

"I guess I will go ahead and tell you about the investigation." I looked at him. "We have security footage from Greer Street. It shows three people heading towards the building and roughly thirty minutes later running from it. At the angle, it is hard to tell exactly what is happening at the Jamison building, but there is a bright light in the background."

"Ah, so they used Greer, not Jamison Avenue to access the building. I knew it couldn't be your guy."

"He is not *my guy*. He's my employee." We weren't dating anymore, so I could call him out for this now without worrying about offending him.

"Sorry, just meant your friend." He flashed a weak smile. "Well, with the video, you know who it is."

"Yes and no."

"I thought you knew who it was."

"I'm getting there. So then there is what happened to Nash."

"Nash? What happened to him?"

"You know he was killed last night?"

"He was what?" Todd shot up and began pacing. "Are you asking if I killed Nash? I did not."

I tried to keep from looking at Detective Upton's car across the street. Thankfully, he hadn't climbed out of it. I was worried he would come over here before I was done.

"Maybe not you personally, but why was Foster at his house? Why was Foster on Greer that night?" Okay, I don't know yet that it was Foster, but I had a feeling, so why not push it?

He stared at me like I slapped him.

"I have no idea why he was at either place. He works for me, but I don't own his spare time."

"He said he was at Nash's for you."

"He told you that?" Todd sat again.

"Yes, he said you wanted him to drop off a cease-and-desist letter."

"For what? Protests? They are annoying but not going to make me stop the project."

That made so much sense. Now I was feeling really stupid. I should have done better research.

"I'm sorry. I just thought—"

"You thought you were going to do a gotcha on me, getting me to confess or something? That's why the cops are parked next to your car." He nodded his head in their direction.

I looked over as my face burned. *Bleep! I was busted.*

"I didn't ask them to come."

"But there they are."

"I just want to solve this. So going off of what Foster had said and you mentioning how they had it out for you, I just thought perhaps … I don't know." My mind was racing. "Um, what about the tools and wood in the Jamison Heights Complex, are those yours? Are they one of your workers'?"

"What tools? What wood?"

"In the front lobby area, or what used to be the front lobby, there is a large toolbox, tools, like hammers and a table saw, then 2x2s and 2x4s leaning against the wall."

"I have no idea." He scratched his head. "I was just there today, and it wasn't there."

"That's weird." I looked at him. "Do you think they could belong to someone on your team?"

"It's possible. They had gone over to put up those no trespassing signs and I guess they could have left it behind. Then sometime between then and today, they picked it up."

We were both quiet for a moment. I guess the tools were not a clue. Darn. I thought that meant it pointed to someone on the project team.

"So, who could it be?" I muttered, not really meaning to say it out loud.

"It's not me, okay? Maybe Foster is the guy, but I am not." He stood again and started to storm off. "I'm sorry I hurt you. That was never my intention. For what it's worth, I do think you are an amazing person, but maybe just a friend. I want this murder solved as much, if not more, than you, because it will help me get the final approvals and funding so I can actually make this building happen."

He looked at me for a second, before hanging his head and walking away.

I sat there with my mixed feelings. For whatever this was, I hadn't been fully in it, but now I felt kind of empty. I think it was more the idea of being in a relationship and Todd had been sweet to me, even if his intentions weren't great.

Would I ever find someone who truly loved me?

Remembering Detective Upton, I looked over. He and Officer Rafferty were walking my way. I looked in the direction Todd had walked, but didn't see him any longer. Thank goodness. I didn't want any more confrontation.

"What happened?" Detective Upton said, gesturing towards City Hall.

"He didn't do it."

"Are you sure?"

"Yeah, I'm sure." I looked at the ground, then up. "He wants it solved too, so he can get more funding for the project."

"He dumped you?" Rafferty blurted out.

My mouth fell open.

"Um, yeah, I guess. Why … or how did you know?"

"Your face. You looked sad."

I touched my face.

"I've known you a long time, Jess." He winked.

"That's true." I looked over at Detective Upton. "Sorry, but yeah, I thought it was Todd. I guess I was wrong."

"I was hoping it was, just because our only suspect is still Marco."

"Yeah, but I don't want it to be anyone I know, even if they just broke up with me." Did it actually count as a breakup? It felt like it, but maybe my feelings were more in the disappointment of not solving the crime.

"Well, I'm glad that it didn't go south on you, at least physically," Detective Upton said. "Sorry about the break-up."

"It's okay."

"Do you have any other names?"

I thought to mention Foster, but my theory had been that he and Todd had plotted against Kimberly, Piper, and Nash which is why Nash had been killed. But that theory was just blown up.

I also didn't mention the security footage yet, because I didn't want to explain how I got it. Plus, if Cullen's friend didn't come through, we couldn't use it anyway. I knew the police department, with their limited resources, didn't have the ability to correct the resolution on the video.

"Nope, nobody."

We all walked back to our cars together. I said goodbye to them and headed home. I needed to study that board again.

When I arrived home, I looked over at Nash's unit. They had removed the crime tape at some point during the day. That meant they had gotten all the clues they needed and were done processing the scene.

That was fast, I thought, but perhaps that could work in my favor.

I looked around the street. No witnesses. Did I dare try to break in? It was not a skill I had, but I thought I could try. How hard could it be?

As I started towards it, a car turned onto our street and pulled to a stop in front of me. It was Mr. Jones, bringing Shayla home. She didn't work today either.

He rolled his window down, and Shayla jumped out with a smile.

"Hey, Mr. Jones. Hi, Shayla." I waved.

"Hey, Jessie. It's so good to see you," Mr. Jones said. "Beverly and I are going to dinner at your place tonight. June and Bev are friends, you know?"

"I did know that. I hope y'all enjoy it."

"We always do. Take care. See you tomorrow, Shayla."

"Thanks, Mr. J!" She waved as he drove away, then turned to me. "You looked like you were up to something when we pulled up. What's going on?" she asked with a giggle.

"Did he notice?"

"If he did, he didn't say anything. But I am right, you were about to do something."

I looked over my shoulder at the now empty unit.

"I was thinking about trying to break in to see if I could find any clues."

"Oh, can you do that? I know you can't legally, but I mean, you know how to break in?"

"No, I wish, but I was going to try."

"Let me put my stuff down and I'll help."

She went inside and came back a moment later. Together, we walked across the street, but then I didn't know what to do.

"Now, what?" she asked.

"Um, let me just check the door. You never know, right?"

I walked up the couple of steps, looking carefully for a security camera, but not seeing one. That was a lucky break. Most people on the block had them. I turned the doorknob, but it didn't budge. Not sure what else to do, I knocked on the door.

I nearly fell down the stairs when, a moment later, it opened. A red-eyed Piper stood there.

"What do you want?"

"I, um, I just wanted to check on you. See if there was anything you needed." Not that I knew she was living there, but then my brain reminded me that I had almost always seen two people going in or out of the unit.

"Not unless you can bring my friend back to life. No. I need nothing."

"I am so sorry to hear. I didn't know him, but he seemed nice." Did he? I only saw him at the protests, but I was being polite.

"We were going to change the world together, but now he is gone."

"I hate to ask, but what happened?"

"He died. Can I go now?"

"Oh, yes, I'm sorry again. If you need anything, I'm across the street."

"Yeah, I know. Why do you think we picked this spot?" She let out a maniacal laugh. "So, we could watch you and Todd."

"Really? I'm so boring."

"Are you though? Crime Fighting Chef." With that, she slammed the door in my face, and I was left stunned. I hadn't been paranoid. I knew I was being watched.

"That was weird," Shayla whispered as we walked back across the street.

"Was it? I can't even tell anymore."

"So, what's for dinner tonight?"

"Stuffed peppers."

"I love stuffed peppers. I had never made them before working for you."

"Oh, yeah?"

"Yeah. You probably already know, but we didn't have a lot of food at home. At least nothing home cooked. It was all frozen pizzas or frozen waffles, all with wonderful freezer burn. I love living here."

"Well, you can stay as long as you want." I gave her a gentle side hug.

"I can't take advantage of you."

"You aren't. Trust me." I smiled. "Do you have homework?"

She burst into a playful laugh.

"You're turning into such a mom. I love it." She grabbed her backpack and swung it onto the kitchen island. "But to answer, yes, I have some."

"I'll start prepping dinner and you do that." I winked.

"Yes, mom. Can I have a snack?"

"Like, you want me to make cookies or something?"

"No, mine are better anyway. I just want an apple or something, and some hot tea."

"Oh, yes, sure."

An hour or so later, I was pulling the peppers from the oven and popping in the garlic bread. She was putting her homework and books back into her bag when Vee and Sawyer came in.

"Hey, honey, we're home," Sawyer announced.

Shayla laughed and ran over to hug them.

"It smells good in here," Vee said.

"Dinner is just out of the oven. Go change and then we can eat."

My phone chimed. It was Cullen.

C: **Video is ready. You are not going to believe who it is.**

Me: **I have a good idea of who it is.**

C: **Then maybe you will not be surprised**

Me: **I really appreciate this.**

I looked over at Shayla.

"What is it?" she asked.

"Cullen sent the video."

She squealed, "who is it?"

"I haven't played it yet. I'm kind of nervous."

"Why?"

"Because of who I think it is."

"You think it is Todd?"

"Not him, but sort of." I took a deep breath, then pulled up the email. "Here we go."

Holding the phone so Shayla could see it, I pushed play. The video started and the once grainy image was crystal clear. Within seconds, the three people came into view. One of them was Nash.

Shayla looked up at me with a tight grimace on her face.

"Is that who you thought?"

"Yep. I need to call Detective Upton now."

But before I could, my phone chimed a text message. It was from Todd.

T: **I think I'm in trouble**

Me: **Why are you telling me?**

T: **Because you were right and I need your help**

Me: **About the murderer? Where are you?**

No answer. It went unread. I don't know why, but I had an uneasy feeling about him. Now, I really needed to call Detective Upton.

Chapter Eighteen

But before I called the detective, I thought I would try Todd. I hit his number on my phone. It rang and rang.

"Come on. Come on. Pick up."

His voicemail answered.

"Bleep!" I hit the button again. Same outcome. "Voicemail. Ugh!"

My throat tightened, and my stomach churned. We might have ended our relationship, but that didn't mean I wanted any harm to come to him.

Vee came downstairs with a huge smile on her face. It faded quickly when she saw me.

"What's wrong?"

"I got the video, and it is who we thought."

"Foster?"

"Yep, along with Nash and Piper."

"Really? Do you think Foster and Piper killed Nash?"

"I do, then Todd sent me a text asking for my help, but he isn't answering his phone now."

"Did you call Detective Upton or Raff?"

"That was my next call."

I hit the button for Upton. It rang and rang. No answer. I stared at my phone for a second.

"That's weird."

"No answer?" Vee asked.

"None. He always answers." I tried again. It rang once.

"Ha-llo?" came a sweet little voice. It had to be Aiden.

"Hi, buddy, this is your friend, Chef Jessica. Is your daddy there?"

"Hi, Chef. Hi, Chef. Cheese?" He loved the pimento cheese at the restaurant.

"Aiden, sweetie, where is daddy?"

I should have just called Rafferty or Perez or even 9-1-1. Any of those wouldn't have me going through the toddler obstacle course, but I trusted Detective Upton with this.

"He sleeping now. Shhhh."

"Aiden, where is mommy?" Time was ticking.

"She with baby Evie."

"Can you take the phone to mommy?"

"Yes."

I heard him scampering through the house, giggling the entire way. Boy, if he wasn't so darn cute, I would be annoyed, but my patience was getting a little thin.

"Momma. Phone. Jess."

"Hello?"

"Hi, Brooke. It's Chef Jessica. Is Rich around?" It felt weird calling him by his first name. I never did that.

"He's napping."

"It's urgent. Can you wake him?"

"Of course, one sec."

His sleepy voice came through the phone. "Who is it?"

"It's Jess. It sounds urgent."

"Jess, what's wrong?" His voice was gravely from just waking.

"I know who the killer, or should I say killers, is. And I think Todd may be in trouble."

"What? Are you sure?"

"I am." I explained the clues that led me here, the text from Todd, including the perfectly clear security footage. "And please don't ask me how I got it, just know that I have it."

"Okay. Did you try to call him?"

"Yes, of course. It keeps going to voicemail."

The pit in my stomach was growing.

"Do you know where he was last?"

"Should have been at work still? City hall."

"Okay, I'm going to call dispatch and get police officers sent. Stay back."

"Okay."

"I mean it, Jess. I can't stop you from driving around town, but I can keep you from going into a potentially active crime scene."

"I won't. We'll just park across the street at the library and wait. Just be witnesses."

"Okay. Thank you."

We hung up. I stared at my phone for a moment.

"I really hope we are wrong, and he just isn't able to answer his phone."

"Yeah, I hope so, too."

Vee grabbed her keys. Shayla started to follow us but stopped in her tracks.

"What about Sawyer? And dinner?" She pointed towards the kitchen.

"Y'all, go. I'll be fine." We turned to see Sawyer coming down the stairs. "This sounds more important. I'll wrap all of this up so you can eat when you get home."

We nodded, then ran out the door. We drove across town as quickly as we could. Vee wasn't the best driver, but somehow, we made it.

She steered the car into an empty spot at the library. City hall looked quiet. Nothing unusual. About a dozen or so cars in the lot. That seemed right for a late Friday afternoon. There was a mother with two young children walking through the rose garden. The youngest stopped to point at a large red rose that was near the end of its life. I couldn't help but remember just a few hours ago, sitting in the center of that park, having the discussion with Todd.

It was so peaceful.

"Uh, maybe we are wrong," Vee said as we watched the family.

"Yes, it is so calm and peaceful here."

We sat for a few minutes, but something just didn't feel right. A police cruiser pulled up at city hall. They rolled into the lot, parking in a designated spot for officers. We saw Rafferty and Roberts get out. They looked around before going inside.

"That's it. Two officers?"

What if I'm wrong? What if this was all a bad prank? Was he mad at me for accusing him of murder, or at least being involved?

Bleep!

We sat for several minutes before Raff and Roberts walked out. Roberts grabbed his radio and looked to be talking. They got back into their car and left.

"That's it. They weren't in there long," Shayla said.

"Well, now what?" Vee asked.

"I don't know. This just doesn't feel right. I can't explain it, but this is wrong."

I opened the car door, getting out. Vee and Shayla followed. Together, we crossed the street and made our way into city hall. It was quiet, with just a few people milling about in the main hall. I looked down one hall and then the other.

"Which way?" Vee whispered.

"I don't know." I looked up at the second floor. "This way."

We headed straight to the stairs. Up here is where the mayor's office and city council had their offices. It wasn't necessarily off limits to the public, but there wasn't anyone else up here at this time. I had only been up here once when Todd brought me to see his office.

I turned left to head down the hall. His office was about halfway down on the right. I knocked at the closed door. No answer. I turned the knob, pushing it open.

My eyes bugged out when I saw what a mess it was. It looked like a tornado had come through. Everything was tossed and flipped. His chair was on its side, his sandscape art that I had admired the last time I was here was shattered on the floor. Shiny sand was scattered all over the floor and mixed with … I let out a gasp. It was blood. Lots of it.

"Is that…?" Vee shrieked. Shayla backed out of the room and stood in the hallway.

"Yes," I grabbed my phone and called Detective Upton.

"Upton."

"Detective, it's Jess. I found blood in Todd's office."

"What? Raff and Roberts didn't find anything."

"They weren't in here very long. Did they even come up to the offices? Todd's is trashed."

"I'm almost there. Stay put. Don't go anywhere else and don't touch anything."

"Yes, sir."

"I'm serious, Jess. I already told you to wait."

I wanted to argue that I had waited until the police had arrived. However, those officers left, so I assumed it was clear to go in.

"I'm sorry. I will."

We hung up. I gave a shrug.

"I guess he isn't happy we came up here."

"He is rarely happy with me until I solve these murders for him."

Shayla was mumbling and bouncing from foot to foot. I went to her, wrapping an arm around her. I guess she was having some PTSD from her family life. Of course, an executive office being trashed was a far cry from her house, but still the emotions were likely the same.

We stood in the hallway, just outside of his office, for roughly ten minutes before footsteps sounded. We turned to see Detective Upton followed by Officers Rafferty and Roberts coming towards us. All three had deep frowns on their faces. I guess the officers didn't like being called out for not doing their job fully.

"In here." I pointed.

They stepped in and immediately Roberts started taking pictures and Upton got on his radio to call into the station. Rafferty looked over his shoulder at me, flashing a sympathetic smile.

"Okay, I need the three of you to wait downstairs. I will be down in a few to ask you questions," Upton said in his authoritative tone.

"Okay." We shuffled our way downstairs, taking seats in the empty waiting room. The sound of them upstairs echoed downstairs, but I couldn't tell what was being said.

Minutes later, more officers arrived and then Upton came downstairs.

"Can I see the video?"

I pulled out my phone, navigated to the video, and then pushed play. He watched expressionlessly. When it ended, he asked me to forward it to him.

"Of course." A few clicks later, he had it.

"You haven't heard anything else from Todd?"

"No, and given the state of his office, are you surprised?"

"Um, no, I admit that doesn't look good."

I fought the urge to say, "*No, duh, Captain Obvious.*" But I kept it to myself.

"Do you have anyone out looking for him?"

"Not yet. It isn't that easy."

"You saw the blood. The smashed up office, right?" Vee asked.

"Yes, we are making a game plan now and will be going to look in a moment. Are there any other clues or anything we should know about?"

I thought about it. Piper was living across from me. There were those tools at the building. I remembered the movement in the empty one behind it.

"Oh, crap, I know where they are!" I blurted. "Greer. In the old Sloane Department store building."

"Really? Why do you say that?"

"I will tell you but don't get mad."

He ran a hand over his face. "I'm sure I'm going to regret promising that, but okay, I promise I won't get mad."

"I was snooping around the Jamison building, but I parked on Greer, going down the alley and in the back door."

"Like we used to when we were kids." Vee laughed, then sobered when Upton shot her a stern look.

"When I was coming out, I swear there was noise coming from that building. More than just a mouse or birds. It was like people were inside of it."

"How could you hear that?"

"It is easy. That block of town is so quiet, almost too quiet. There aren't people living or working within that whole block, especially now with the Jamison Complex on hold."

"Okay, that helps." He grabbed his radio, calling dispatch as he headed upstairs to get the officers.

"Should we go?" Shayla asked.

"He would hate it," Vee said, a giggle escaping. "Let's do it."

"But one thing," I said.

"What's that?" they asked.

"We should run!"

With that, we took off as fast as we could out the door and to Vee's car. We were out of the parking lot before any of the officers knew what happened. Vee steered us quickly the roughly ten blocks to Jamison.

"Let's check the Jamison building first, just in case," I said when we got close.

Vee drove slowly, then stopped across from the burned building.

"It looks quiet here," she said.

"It does, but... Oh dang, do you see that? The building is on fire." I pointed. I grabbed my phone and called 9-1-1. No time to get the officers involved. If Todd was inside, we needed the fire put out now.

After I'd hung up with the 9-1-1 operator, we sat there. A few seconds after I hung up, Shayla made a strangled sound.

"That fire is not coming from this building on Jamison. It looks like it's behind it." She pointed.

We looked more carefully. Sure enough, it was coming from behind it.

"Oh, dang, I think you're right." I called back, giving them the correct building.

"Should we drive around to Greer?" Vee asked, poised to do just that.

"No, no. We should stay here." I knew Detective Upton was already going to be mad that we came over here without him.

We didn't have to wait long before the firetrucks arrived, followed closely by nearly all of Dashwood Police Department. Detective Upton came to our car.

"Seriously? You ran off?"

"Yeah, but if we hadn't, it would have been even longer before the firetrucks would get here. Y'all would just now be arriving and then you'd have to call them. But there they are putting out the fire now."

He hung his head. "Fine. You got me there, but I can't support this. Now stay here until we clear the scene. Then I want to talk to you."

I nodded, and he turned to get to work.

Most of the action was happening on Greer, so all we could do was sit here and wait. It was roughly an hour later, when Rafferty came running over to the car, a huge smile on his face.

"Well, good job, Crime Fighting Chef. You saved the building and Todd Barber, the mayor, and Kimberly Gibbs."

"Foster had all of them?"

"Yes."

"How did he kidnap three people without anyone knowing? And more importantly why?"

"We are still trying to figure out all the pieces and motive but looks like he lured Kimberly here. Then grabbed the mayor from her house. Todd was a little harder for him. As you saw in the office, there was a fight and then he had to get him out of the building without alerting anyone what was happening."

"And does this mean Marco is cleared?"

"Yep, we already have the call in to his lawyer. He is free." Raff smiled at me. "You did it again. Maybe you should have been a detective."

"Oh, ha, no. This was just dumb luck."

"Four times is not just luck, Jess." He looked at me, then at the other two ladies. "Well, I'm going to get back to it, but Upton wanted me to let you know it's over and everyone is safe."

"Thank you."

We watched as he ran back across the street.

"He likes you," Shayla said.

"Raff? No." I laughed, but then I really thought about it on our drive home. Maybe he did. Dang.

Chapter Nineteen

It has been a few weeks since I last saw Todd. He had burns and a head injury, but he was recovering well. I had visited him in the hospital the next day.

"Oh, hey Jess." He sat up.

"I brought you some chicken and dumplings." I handed him the bag.

"Yum. Thanks. I love this."

"How are you feeling?"

"Crispy and a little lightheaded." He chuckled.

"I bet."

"Thank you for your work on this. I can't believe it was Foster. You were so right about him."

"Do you know why he kidnapped all of you?"

"He had it out for me after one of my past projects. He had lived in one of the buildings that my company renovated. He felt it was subpar work, but when the civil suit was ruled in my favor, he was angered. I didn't even know he was one of the plaintiffs on that case."

"I read about them, but didn't know he was part of that."

"Yeah, those were a mess, but all of them were settled in my favor. No evidence that I used subpar materials or cheap labor. I have a dozen successful projects with only a few that people complained about."

"That's good, but then why had he held such a grudge? That seems so random?"

"Who knows how people's minds work? He simply said to the police that I wasn't fit to run a project and that I used subpar materials. Weak, right?"

"Yeah, very weak." I paused. "What about kidnapping Kimberly and the mayor?"

"He said that it was because the mayor supported this project."

"That's it? So petty."

"It really is." He smiled at me. "Kimberly was because he didn't like the direction she was leading the Dashwood Beautification Organization. He thought they should fight harder for environmental rights and climate change, more protests. He wanted to take charge of the group."

"Wow. Is that why he killed Nash?"

"I guess so, but you may need to ask the police about that. They didn't give me the scoop on that. Just those parts that were directly related to my case."

I nodded.

"Did he say, or did the police mention, why he killed Zachary Boyd? He had no connection to the project," I asked.

"When he grabbed me, I asked him. He said that man was just in the wrong place at the wrong time."

"So, he hadn't been a target, just in the building when they arrived, so they killed him?" I was stunned but also had thought that might be the case.

"Yeah, sad to say, that is poor Zach's only crime, so to speak."

I processed what he said. I'm sure that would sadden Marco, but at least he now had some closure, and his friend would now get justice.

"Well, I'm glad that you are on the mend. I'll let you rest now." I smiled, turning to leave.

"Jess, wait." He sat forward, reaching for my hand. I didn't take it, so he let his hand drop. "For what it's worth, I am very sorry for hurting you. That was never my intention, and like I said yesterday, I did find you interesting. I hope we can be friends in some way."

I looked at him with the ugly gash on his head and the bright red burn marks on his arms, neck, and face. Honestly, I don't know that I was necessarily hurt by him so much as I was mad at myself for dating someone I wasn't even sure about. But I was starting to like him there at the end.

"Yeah, I think we can."

His eyes brightened, and a huge smile spread across his face.

"Well, hot dog. I'm glad you forgive me," Todd clapped.

"Yeah, well, I don't bring just anyone my chicken and dumplings." I winked. "Well, take care."

With that, I left. I stared at myself in the mirror now as I was getting ready to head over to the groundbreaking for the Jamison Heights Complex.

They finally got all the funding and approvals without the Dashwood Beautification Organization standing in the way. In fact, there was a new initiative on the city council's agenda to create a park and it would be on Greer instead. They were going to tear down the old Sloane Department store after Foster burned half of it to the ground.

"What does one wear to a groundbreaking?" I mumbled.

"What you have on looks great," Sawyer said from the door. Riley smiled by his side.

"You do."

"You think?" I looked at them in the reflection.

The dark green A-line dress was not my usual style. I had some nude heels on. Again, not my typical style, but Todd had warned me that I would be called up onto the stage. I wanted to look a little more professional than a Neal Barney t-shirt and jeans.

Granny and Auntie Rita had been more than happy to go shopping with me again, especially when I told them what the outfit was for.

"We are so very proud of you, Jessie!" Auntie Rita had said.

"We really are, Mija." Granny agreed.

Vee came around Sawyer and Riley to check out my outfit.

"Oh, wow, Jess! You look gorgeous." She smiled.

Shayla came into the room in her brand-new maroon dress with black floral print. I had taken her along shopping too. We bought her a whole new wardrobe as well. I wanted her to feel special.

"Are we ready?" she asked, a huge grin on her face.

"Yes."

We headed over to Jamison Avenue, but we couldn't get close. They had it blocked, but a friendly face was directing traffic.

"Well, hey, gang," Rafferty said, when we pulled up next to him. "Guest of honor has special VIP parking. Park in the lot marked VIP."

He moved the barrier so we could drive through.

"You look nice, Jess." He smiled, then waved as we drove past.

"He really does have a crush on you," Shayla teased.

I laughed and looked behind us. He was standing there, still watching our car. I waved. He waved back.

"Yep, it looks like it," I said.

We parked and walked to join the ceremony in front of the building. It was large. I saw lots of familiar faces, including my grandmother and aunt. They waved for us to join them.

"Hi, kids," Granny Ines said, giving us each a hug. "I'm so proud of you, Jessie."

"Thanks."

We settled in next to them, but I heard someone calling me.

"Jess, Jess!" It was Todd from the stage. "Come up here."

"Oh, no, it's okay. I'll wait for the start of the ceremony."

"No, we have a seat for you up here." He gestured.

"Go, Jessie," Granny said. I couldn't argue with her.

I stood on wobbly legs and joined the others on the stage. The crowd cheered when they saw me, even though the ceremony hadn't started yet.

My face burned as I looked out and waved at them. I loved being behind the scenes. This was not my thing, but here I was to support my friend and the town.

A lady next to me leaned over, offering her hand. I took it giving it a shake.

"We haven't officially met, I'm Kimberly Gibbs, and I wanted to offer my sincere thank you for helping to save me."

"Nice to meet you." I smiled. "No thanks necessary, I was just doing what any decent person would."

Her online picture didn't do her justice in the best way. She looked younger, prettier in person, even with the burn marks from the fire, like both Todd and Mayor Lackland had. Thankfully, they were all healing well.

"Oh, don't be modest. You're a true hero. My family thanks you." She pointed to a man with two young girls. The girls giggled and waved from their seats.

I couldn't form words, seeing those little girls. She could have died and left them all behind. I was so glad that I had saved that family.

Mayor Patricia Lackland stood, walking to the podium.

"Welcome, citizens of Dashwood." She began. "We are here today to kick off the Jamison Heights Complex project. A mixed-use building with boutique stores, restaurants, and residential apartments. It will bring new life to this block of Dashwood and offer new opportunities."

The crowd cheered. She smiled.

"Now, I would like to introduce our project leader, Todd Barber." She turned, clapping.

"Thank you, Mayor and town of Dashwood. It has taken us a long time to get here, but we are finally here."

The crowd applauded loudly again. They were excited. That made sitting up here at least a little easier.

"But it wouldn't have been possible without our special guest, Jessica Vasquez, or as most of you know her, Chef Jessica, owner and chef of The Crock Pot."

The crowd sprang to their feet. My face warmed as I realized all this craziness was for me.

"I want to call her forward now." He turned, gesturing for me to join him. I stood and shuffled over. "Now, I want to thank you from the bottom of my heart. Without you, I would not be here. The mayor and Kimberly Gibbs from the Dashwood Beautification Organization wouldn't be here. So, from myself and the town of Dashwood, we would like to present you with this award."

Mayor Lackland and Kimberly Gibbs stepped forward. The mayor was holding a plaque with a large brass key on it and an engraved plate underneath it. She smiled brightly.

"I owe you so much more than this, but Chef Jessica, here is the key to the city and a sincere thank you for my life, and Todd's and Kim's. You are a true treasure to Dashwood."

She handed me the plaque and shook my hand. A photographer was wildly snapping pictures of the whole scene.

"Do you want to say a few words?" Todd asked.

"Um," I stepped to the podium. "I just want to thank you all for the support of my business and for this honor. I didn't do it for this, but to help my friends."

I smiled down at Marco and Selene. They were holding hands, back together, and happy with the mystery solved. Marco was going to continue seeing a therapist, but he was back to normal with all of this behind him.

I nodded and stepped back. The crowd stood again, cheering, yelling their thank yous and support, and clapping wildly. It was a lot.

Todd calmed everyone, so we could continue. I am not sure what was said for the rest of the ceremony as I took my seat again and stared at the plaque. I traced the key with my finger. This was amazing.

After the ceremony ended, there was a reception and lots of handshakes, photos, and congratulations. All I could think was that it was just another day in the life of the Crime Fighting Chef.

THE END

Before you go: If you loved Dumplings and Disaster, be sure to visit my website to sign up for my newsletter (if you haven't already) and to stay up to date on new releases and other bookish things. When signing up, you will receive **Chef Jessica's Alphabet Soup Recipe** as a free gift. I have "had" it, it is yummy. (Okay, so obviously, it is my recipe, but still, I recommend it!)

Continue to the next section for this book's recipe!

www.ejwheltonwrites.com

Recipe:

I love chicken and dumplings. I am including both the chicken soup part and the dumplings recipes; however, you can use your own favorite chicken soup recipe and then add the dumplings to that one. Or you can make my favorite (and simple) recipe.

Chicken Soup:

4-6 skinless chicken thighs (or really about 1 ½ pounds of chicken)
8 cups of water
1 large onion, chopped
3 stalks of celery, chopped
2 cups (or roughly 4) carrots, sliced
2 cloves garlic or 2 teaspoons of "jar-lic" (the minced in the jar)
1 teaspoon thyme (ground)
Salt (to taste)
Pepper (to taste)

Instructions:
Add everything except carrots and thyme to the 8 cups of water. Boil until chicken is cooked (Roughly 20 minutes after it boils, depending on size of chicken). Remove chicken then debone and shred.

Put chicken back into the pot. Add carrots and thyme. Boil until carrots are tender.

Dumplings:

2 cups all-purpose flour
1 1/2 tablespoon baking powder
1 teaspoon black pepper (optional)
1 teaspoon salt
1 cup milk
4 tablespoons butter, melted

Instructions:
Mix all dry ingredients together and then add the milk and butter, mixing until you have a batter. It should be like a thin paste.

When your soup is ready, ensure you bring it to a rolling boil and have a lid handy for your pot.

Put a spoon full (or a scoop) of dumpling into the boil, continue until you have used all the batter, cover and boil for 10 minutes. The key is the boil, it should be a nice steady rolling boil before dropping the dumplings.

If you do it right, your broth will be a nice thick broth and your dumplings will be nice and fluffy.

Good luck and enjoy!

Author note:

What to say about this one? I don't know. It was a struggle to get it to the finish line this time. I knew the story, knew what it needed to be, but my day job has been a little extra stressful lately. I was just at burnout.

And I think it is okay to share that.

Life happens. We gather ourselves and move forward anyway.

I want to thank my editing team for their hard work on this one! It is because of you that this has happened again.

Thank you to the veterans. To those who served with me, those that came before me, and those who are serving now. This story wasn't focused on the military, but I wanted a soft nod. Get help for your mental health, PTSD, or loneliness.

As always, I couldn't do this without you, dear reader. So thank you once again for the support and for reading my stories. I have many more to come with Chef Jessica and friends. I also have two other series and a few standalone books, just in case you are interested.

www.ejwheltonwrites.com